WILLIAMS

A STREETCAR NAMED DESIRE

NOTES

WILSON F. ENGEL, III, Ph. D.

COLES notes

OTABIND

Bound to stay open

Publisher's Note

Otabind (Ota-bind). This book has been bound using the patented Otabind process. You can open this book at any page, gently run your finger down the spine, and the pages will lie flat.

ABOUT COLES NOTES

COLES NOTES have been an indispensible aid to students on five continents since 1948.

COLES NOTES are available for a wide range of individual literary works. Clear, concise explanations and insights are provided along with interesting interpretations and evaluations.

Proper use of COLES NOTES will allow the student to pay greater attention to lectures and spend less time taking notes. This will result in a broader understanding of the work being studied and will free the student for increased participation in discussions.

COLES NOTES are an invaluable aid for review and exam preparation as well as an invitation to explore different interpretive paths.

COLES NOTES are written by experts in their fields. It should be noted that any literary judgement expressed herein is just that — the judgement of one school of thought. Interpretations that diverge from, or totally disagree with any criticism may be equally valid.

COLES NOTES are designed to supplement the text and are not intended as a substitute for reading the text itself. Use of the NOTES will serve not only to clarify the work being studied, but should enhance the reader's enjoyment of the topic.

ISBN 0-7740-3793-8

COLES PUBLISHING COMPANY
TORONTO—CANADA
PRINTED IN CANADA

Manufactured by Webcom Limited
Cover finish: Webcom's Exclusive **Duracoat**

CONTENTS

TENNESSEE WILLIAMS LIFE AND WORKS

Biographical Sketch

Tennessee Williams (1911-1983) was born Thomas Lanier Williams in Columbus, Missouri. Some time during 1939 he took for himself the name "Tennessee."

He used events from his childhood as material for some of his plays. Especially significant for him were his sister Rose's schizophrenia, his mother's Southern background and social attitudes, and the rough and even brutal manner of his father a clothing salesman who spent much of his time on the road. Williams had a special fondness for his maternal grandfather, an Episcopal minister, to whom he dedicated his only volume of collected poetry, *In the Winter of Cities* (1956).

As a youth Williams was sickly and sensitive. He turned to writing early as a means of dealing with a home life full of conflict, illusion, and pain. His first writing to be accepted for publication was the story "The Vengeance of Nitocris." *Weird Tales* magazine paid him $35 for it in 1928.

He attended the University of Missouri between 1931 and 1933. Because he failed a military training course, his father made him withdraw. His father found him a job as a clerk with International Shoe, where Williams worked for two years while continuing to write at night.

In 1935 he suffered what may have been a nervous breakdown and quit his dreary job. That same year, the first play in which he had a hand was performed by the Memphis Garden Players in Memphis, Tennessee. Its name was *Cairo, Shanghai, Bombay*! It was a farce and its success led him to decide on a career as a writer. He returned to school, attending Washington University in St. Louis in 1936 and 1937. He was profoundly affected when in 1937 his sister Rose's schizophrenia worsened to the point that her doctors performed a prefrontal lobotomy on her brain. It was one of the first to be done in the United States.

Williams left Missouri to complete his Bachelor's degree at the University of Iowa in 1938. He graduated while the United States was in the grip of the Great Depression of the 1930s, and work was scarce. One of the few safe havens for writers was the

Work Projects Administration Writers Project, established by the United States Government in 1935. But the Project rejected him on the grounds that his work did not have "social content." He drifted for a period, taking odd jobs where he could find them and continuing to write.

By Williams' own account, the first important recognition of his work came when he received a major grant, a Rockefeller fellowship, to write *Battle of Angels.* Its first performance in 1940 marked the beginning of what was to become Williams' tradition of outraging theatre audiences. This initial failure later became, in rewritten form, *Orpheus Descending* (1957). As this case shows, Williams often reworked an idea in a succession of forms at various times.

In 1943, through a friend's influence, Williams was offered a six-month contract to write film scripts for Metro-Goldwyn-Mayer. He was unable to write a satisfactory script for the actress Lana Turner, and instead tried to sell his employers a film idea called "The Gentleman Caller." His bosses rejected it along with Williams' contract extension. In its final form this rejected idea came to Broadway as *The Glass Menagerie* (1945), which won the New York Drama Critics' Circle Award as the best play of the year. *Menagerie* was in part based on the life of his unfortunate sister Rose and is often called "Williams' gentlest play."

Williams did not allow early success to ruin his writing. He followed *Menagerie* with *A Streetcar Named Desire,* which was first performed at the Ethel Barrymore Theater. It was an immediate success, running for 855 performances and earning Williams his first Pulitzer Prize for drama in 1948. From 1945 to 1962 Williams produced a phenomenal number of high-quality plays. *Summer and Smoke* (1948) was a revision of an earlier play, *"The Yellow Rose"* and later was itself revised as *Eccentricites of a Nightingale* (1964). *The Rose Tattoo* (1951) and *Camino Real* (1953 — a revision of an earlier one-act play) were followed by *Cat on a Hot Tin Roof* (1955) which ran for 694 performances and earned Williams another Pulitzer Prize.

Williams' personal life included both sadness and accolades. He was faced with the death of his personal secretary in 1955 and with the death of his father in 1957. In that year, as he grew increasingly depressed, he entered psychoanalysis. That was the same year *Orpheus Descending* appeared. Among his later plays are: *Garden District* (1958 — two one-act plays which include *Suddenly Last Summer);* the immensely popular *Sweet Bird of Youth* (1959), which held the stage for 383 performances and, like all of Williams' plays, toured extensively and has been widely performed; *Period of Adjustment* (1960), *Night of the Iguana* (1961); and *The Milk Train Doesn't Stop Here Anymore* (1962). In the opinion of some critics, Williams' last great play was *Night of the Iguana,* but he continued to write until his death, by accidental choking, in 1983.

Other plays he wrote in the 1960s include *Slapstick Tragedy* (1965 — two short plays), *The Seven Descendents of Myrtle* (1968 — revised in 1975 as *Kingdom of Earth),* and *In the Bar of a Tokyo Hotel* (1969). In 1969 Williams became a convert to Roman Catholicism at the urging of his brother.

After 1969 Williams wrote, among others plays, *Small Craft Warnings* (1972), *The Red Devil Battery Sign* (1975), *Vieux Carre* (1977), *Creve Coeur* (1978), and *Clothes for a Summer Hotel* (1980).

In addition to plays, Williams wrote poems, including those in the volume *In the Winter of Cities* (1956). He also wrote numerous short stories, some of which were later reworked as plays. His story collections include *Our Arm and Other Stories* (1948), *Hard Candy: A Book of Stories* (1954), and *The Knightly Quest* (1968). He also wrote numerous screenplays which include *Baby Doll* (1956), *The Glass Menagerie* (1950), *A Streetcar Named Desire* (1951), *The Rose Tattoo* (1955 — collaborated with Gore Vidal), *Suddenly Last Summer* (1959), *The Fugitive Kind* (1950), and *Boom* (1968 — based on *Milk Train).*

Williams also wrote a novel, *The Roman Spring of Mrs. Stone,* and his autobiographical *Memoirs.* But his plays, particularly those performed before 1962, are the basis for his place in American literary history. Because of his stature as one of the foremost American playwrights, many interviews with him exist, both in print and on tape.

Williams was influenced by a host of other dramatists, among them Eugene O'Neill (1888-1953), perhaps the greatest American playwright; Anton Chekhov (1860-1904), a Russian who wrote for the Moscow Art Theatre; George Bernard Shaw

(1856-1950), the most outstanding modern British playwright; Luigi Pirandello (1867-1936), a Sicilian-born playwright of intellectual and grotesquely humourous plays; and Johan August Strindberg (1849-1912), the Swedish dramatist who used dreams, symbols, and mysticism in his work. Williams' great strength as a playwright lies in his incisiveness in presenting human conflict on the stage. In this, he has a power all his own.

Williams also owes debts to D. H. Lawrence (1855-1930), about whom Williams wrote the play *I Rise in Flame, Cried the Phoenix* (1959), and to two Southern writers. The first of these, William Faulkner (1897-1962), was one of the greatest of Southern novelists, and a winner of the Nobel Prize for Literature. The second, Carson McCullers (1917-1967), a personal friend of Williams, wrote short stories about the effects of human isolation and alienation. Hart Crane (1899-1932), an outstanding young American poet who committed suicide, was a strong influence on Williams. The epigram for *A Streetcar Named Desire* is by Crane. In the case of McCullers, as with Williams' other contemporaries, the influence went both ways.

The degree of Williams' influence on world drama has not yet been carefully measured, but his strong influence on the American, Edward Albee (1928-), and on Harold Pinter (1930-), the British playwright, is easy to see. In his time Williams' only American equal as a writer of important, serious drama was Arthur Miller (1915-), author of *Death of a Salesman* (1949) and *The Crucible* (1953). Miller's plays are more concerned with social problems and intellectual concepts.

From the start Williams probed the darker side of human nature, the vulnerability of human beings with all their sensitivities and illusions. He points out the viciousness of human beings when they sense a difference or alienation in another. He shows the irony in how all men and women want desperately to communicate in a society, even when its taboos ensure a destructive battle for domination. In Williams' plays, madness and sometimes death is often the lot of the loser.

Williams was a ruthless analyst of the American psyche and an exorcist of illusions. He was frequently criticised for how he used violence, especially in his treatment of sexual themes, but the violence is essential to his message, and at his best, his statements about the human condition ring true. Plays like

Streetcar, Menagerie, Cat on a Hot Tin Roof, and *Night of the Iguana* resonate beyond the confines of the period that produced them.

Williams showed a courage in dealing with social problems which, in his day, was shocking. He deals with contemporary issues such as the place of women in society, homosexuality and its social acceptance, and the plight of battered wives. Like the modern-day television dramas on suicide, child abuse and wife battering, his plays brought social problems out of the darkness of collective repression into the light of collective anger and appraisal. Williams was one of the first American dramatists to stir the conscience of his nation. But Williams' drama was not about issues only. The philosophical and even mystical nature of Williams' work can be even more frightening than its social content.

Williams spoke not just for society's unfortunate misfits — he also spoke for the conformists. He speaks to us about the inherent loneliness of modern life, the tendency of individuals to approach damaging or fatal alienation, the withdrawal from ultimate questions, the attraction of ill-considered ideals. The fragility of Williams' dramatic world is hidden by its outward brutality. Like other perceptive writers who took the South as their theme, Williams realized something universal: that the brutal and unfeeling surfaces of people's lives mirrors a pathetic and often hopeless striving — a desire that lacks direction, and a fascination with escape and rest through madness, sexual intercourse, and the grave.

A STREETCAR NAMED DESIRE
Introduction

From the time of its first performance in 1947, *A Streetcar Named Desire* has been controversial. It has defied any of the standard classifications for a dramatic work — tragedy, melodrama, and even grotesque comedy have been suggested for it, and each has some justification. Its subject matter has been criticised for its brutality. Its depiction of American figures has been the subject of many psychological analyses, many of them treating Williams' characters as abnormal rather than normal. Yet against the hostility of moralists, and against the criticism of people who ignore the play's sensitivity to social problems or issues, the play has had almost universal acceptance in performance. It was acknowledged almost immediately after its first stage run to be a classic of American literature.

Stanley Kowalski and Blanche DuBois, for all the brutal simplicity of the former and the baffling complexity of the latter, are two of the towering characters in drama. Their roles are coveted by actors and actresses worldwide. After the play appeared in print, it became clear that Williams' art involved not only powerful portrayal of character but also poetic and powerful language — a language that transformed the language of the American stage.

The roots of *Streetcar* are most easily found in Williams' own earlier play *The Glass Menagerie* (1945), which Williams called a "memory play" before the term became fashionable. As in the works of the Scandinavian playwright Henrik Ibsen (1828-1906), memory plays a major role in Williams' work. It is often shown to be a hidden or partially hidden destroyer whose destructive power is triggered by conflict. The term "memory play" is not a generally recognized dramatic term like "tragedy," "comedy," or "farce." But many playwrights since 1945 have explored the form.

Streetcar, like many good plays, derives its strength from its action and what that action suggests about the human condition. Though Williams does not stay firm to dramatic precedents or rules, he does display a vast knowledge of dramatic history, and he uses the entire range of drama in constructing his plays. Williams borrowed a great many devises and themes from Greek tragedy, Renaissance English drama, Restoration English comedy, and Twentieth-Century Spanish drama. One of the reasons that Williams seems like such a fresh and original talent is that he understood the origins of theatrical power and how to make them vital for his own place and time.

As the epigram to the play indicates, Williams was also a good reader of poetry. His literary tastes were wide and varied, and he studied the major writers in all genres, but most of all in poetry. His transcribed interviews are poetic both in language and in conception, and he wrote poetry that he published separate from the rest of his work. The poetry in Williams' plays is the poetry not of stanzas but of single lines and phrases and of measured use of symbols. Part of Williams' strategy in using language is not to stress too much a play's moments of quiet, reflection, or eloquence.

He has often been compared to T. S. Eliot (1888-1965), who wrote what is now seen as a classic poem in world literature, *The Waste Land*, but he has none of Eliot's exagerated concern for the expanded thought or image. His debt to Eliot is seen in his choice of themes like alienation, the breaking of myths and dreams, and decay — not in his language.

Hart Crane, with his broken eloquence and sometimes dubious imagery, and with his tragic absorption with his work, had a profound influence on Williams which extended to how he modelled his characters and chose his themes and language. Though not written in verse, free or otherwise, *Streetcar* has the density and power of poetry. In performance it rushes forward relentlessly. Many of its effects are emotional rather than intellectual. The rush of Williams' tempo is like that of jazz music and shares the same frenzy as the music he chose for the stage directions of this play.

But Williams' artistic structure is not spontaneous, even though it seems too energetic to be calculated. For a full appreciation of Williams' art, the reader must realize how very deliberate Williams' method of creation was. Williams' inspiration springs from his grasp of the human condition, but he modelled his plays with enormous care. To fully understand *Streetcar,* you must approach it as if it were a poem, and give careful attention to every word and gesture.

Williams drank from a rich literary tradition that included European as well as American works. He constructed powerful and evocative scenes, and fused lyrical and symbolic language with often brutal character portrayal. He lay open the wounds of his society, ruthlessly and without pretension. In doing all of that, Williams surpasses any dramatist in the early post-war tradition with the exception of his contemporary Arthur Miller, author of *The Crucible* (1953).

The first run of *Streetcar* was a major event in the history of American theatre. Coming after *The Glass Menagerie, Streetcar* took America by storm and gained world acclaim. Even though it broke all the rules of polite drama, it made an irresistible statement about the American psyche. Its continued popularity suggests that the statement goes beyond the confines of post-war America and New Orleans and into the human condition, with its fragile illusions and brutal intentions.

Plot Summary

Blanche DuBois arrives in the Elysian Fields district of New Orleans in early May. From the start she is shown to be very different from the people of the lower-class neighborhood where her brother-in-law Stanley Kowalski lives with her pregnant sister Stella. She has brought all her possessions — including her papers and mementos — in a trunk and plans to stay for a while. After an uneasy reunion with her sister, Blanche confesses that Belle Reve, their family's estate, has been lost. She implies that Stella left her to do the dirty work of tending to the last of the relatives as they died. Stanley meets Blanche and immediately demonstrates that while he is crude and vulgar, he is also virile and knows his own mind. The next evening, when he discovers that Belle Reve has been lost, he accuses Blanche of squandering the family's fortune which, according to the state's law, should be partly his. Blanche, denying this, gives him all the papers relating to the estate. In the process, Stanley tells Blanche that Stella is pregnant.

Blanche and Stella return from a restaurant to find that a poker game involving Stanley and his friends Pablo, Steve and Mitch is in full swing. Blanche is interested in Mitch and tries to entertain him, but Stanley becomes angry and throws a radio out the window. When Stella attempts to stop the poker match he meets her with abuse, and the other men must restrain him. He seems to be temporarily insane. Meanwhile Stella escapes upstairs and the men put Stanley under the shower. In spite of all this violence, Stella later comes down from her refuge in the Hubbells' flat in response to Stanley's half self-indulgent and half-repentant animal cries.

The entire poker sequence disturbs Blanche so much she can't sleep at all that night. The next morning Blanche is appalled that her sister is unconcerned at her husband's behaviour. Blanche dreams up an escape plan and begins to draft a letter to a former beau named Shep Huntleigh who, she thinks, will provide the money for the sisters' escape. Finally, Blanche says exactly what she thinks of Stanley and his friends — that they are all disgusting and live like animals — a diatribe which Stanley overhears on the porch. In answer to Blanche's appeal to decency, Stella embraces him warmly when he reappears.

Mitch, Stanley's poker friend, asks Blanche out on a date. Stanley now does some checking on Blanche's background and lets her know he has spoken to a man named Shaw who seems to have known about her when she lived at the Hotel Flamingo, a seedy hotel in Laurel. Shaken by this news, Blanche becomes almost hysterical while talking with Stella. Later, when a young newspaper collector happens to come by, she kisses him on the mouth, just before Mitch arrives for their date. She greets Mitch as if nothing has happened. The date is, however, depressing for both of them, and when they return to the flat, they have a hard time communicating with each other. Finally, Blanche tells Mitch about the suicide of her young husband Allan. In sympathy, Mitch takes her in his arms and suggests they may be able to help each other in their loneliness.

In September Blanche's birthday party is ruined by Stanley, who by now has gathered a lot of information about Blanche's life in Laurel. Stanley has told Mitch everything he has discovered, and as a result Mitch does not come to the party. Further, Stanley has bought Blanche a one-way Greyhound bus ticket back to Laurel. He gives it to her as a present just when she is most vulnerable. When Stella reproaches him for his cruelty, he reminds her proudly of how he brought her down from her lofty pedestal. She suddenly has her first labor pains and asks to be taken to the hospital.

That same night Mitch appears in work clothes, unwashed and unshaven. He has verified what Stanley told him about Blanche and wants to see her in the harsh light of reality. He also wants to have sex with her even though he has now decided that he will definitely not marry her since she is not fit to be taken into the same house as his mother. Blanche gets rid of him by crying "Fire!" She then begins packing, drinking steadily while she does. She stops only to dress up in a white satin evening gown and rhinestone tiara. She fantasizes that Shep Huntleigh has sent her a telegram. Stanley makes an ominous appearance, having been sent home from the hospital where Stella is having his baby. Methodically and with an air of ritual he prepares himself and then rapes Blanche, who tries frantically to escape the inevitable.

A few weeks after the rape, Blanche is prepared for visitors by Eunice and Stella. Though Blanche thinks it is Shep Huntleigh who is coming, these visitors are really personnel from the state mental institution. The men play poker while Blanche, now more than ever a tragically disturbed person, confronts her destiny and is taken away to the asylum. Stella, who has agreed to her sister's being committed to the state institution, receives her new baby from Eunice as a consolation.

Characters in the Play

Blanche DuBois

A sensitive and cultured woman from a decayed Southern aristocratic family. Her loss of the family estate (called Belle Reve which is French for "beautiful dream"), of her reputation and of her job as an English teacher all force her to seek refuge in a lower-class flat with her sister and brother-in-law. The two-room dwelling is full of violence; her pretensions and illusions are systematically stripped away there by her relentless brother-in-law. She progressively loses her sanity until by the end of the play, after her brother-in-law has raped her, she is committed to an asylum.

Stella (DuBois) Kowalski

Blanche's pregnant sister married Stanley Kowalski who is beneath her social class. She loves her brutal husband and assents to having her sister put in an asylum after Blanche tells her that Stanley raped her.

Stanley Kowalski

Stella's husband is a brutal and insensitive but virile man who relentlessly tears away the veils of illusion of his visiting sister-in-law Blanche. He finally has sex with her on the day when his wife, whom he alternately brutalizes and adores, is giving birth to their baby.

Harold ("Mitch") Mitchell

One of Stanley's poker buddies and former fellow soldiers, he becomes smitten with Blanche and at first wants to marry her. But when Stanley informs him about her past he spurns her, cutting off her last hope of marriage and happiness.

Eunice Hubbell

The Kowalskis' upstairs neighbor, friend, and foil to Stella. Her relationship with her husband Steve is even more turbulent than that of the Kowalskis. She seems to be the most violent mate in her marriage.

Steve Hubbell

Eunice's brow-beaten (and possibly cheating) husband, poker companion and foil (or opposite type) for Stanley.

Pablo Gonzales

Another poker companion of Stanley.

A Negro Woman

The Kowalski's neighbor in this racially-mixed area in the melting pot of New Orleans.

A Doctor

This character comes to take Blanche to the asylum at the end of the play.

A Nurse

This matron assists the doctor in taking Blanche to the asylum.

A Young Collector

Blanche toys with this boy at the very time she is waiting for Mitch to show up for a date. He is an immediate example of Blanche's rumored fondness for very young males.

A Blind Mexican Woman

She is turned away by Blanche who by then cannot be helped, and is virtually a stage symbol — selling symbols of death, the tin funeral flowers.

Mrs. Mitchell

(Mitch's mother) is ailing, offstage. Her doting son takes care of her, and in return she worries about him.

Shep Huntleigh

Blanche's image of a wealthy and successful hero — a modern-day knight in shining armour. She desperately then insanely fantasizes that he will come to take her away from the sordidness and misery of her present life. To her, he symbolizes a protected world of wealth and care.

Shaw

Stanley and Mitch's informant about Blanche's reputation in Laurel.

Allan

This sensitive young poet became Blanche's husband when both of them were very young. When his homosexuality became known to her, he committed suicide horribly. He forms a complex memory for her, one to which she repeatedly returns in the play.

Kiefaber

This merchant from Laurel verifies for Mitch the rumors about Blanche's past.

Graves

The school principal who fired Blanche from his staff following her alleged improprieties with a seventeen-year-old boy student.

Mac

One of Stanley's lower-class bowling friends.

Summaries and Commentaries

EPIGRAM

The epigram for the printed versions of *Streetcar* is from Hart Crane's *"The Broken Tower."* It serves to introduce the major themes in the play through its symbolic images of "the broken world," "the visionary company of love," "An instant in the wind," "each desperate choice." Through the language of this excerpt, a mood is established and a tone of serious intent is evoked. It also has the tone of an autobiography. It suggests a personal witness entering a world very like the play's Elysian Fields with its desperation, its fading hopes, and its grotesque abnormalities of language, personal relationships, and values.

Crane is an interesting choice since he, like Allan in the *Streetcar,* committed suicide. In 1932, while returning home from Mexico after a futile attempt to write an epic poem, Crane jumped from a passenger ship and drowned. Williams' use of Crane's poem may also suggest a deep connection, at least in Williams' mind, between Crane and himself. Williams had gone to Mexico to revive his creativity and there produced *The Poker Night,* which later became *Streetcar.* Crane's lifelong anguish as an alcoholic and homosexual may also have evoked Williams' sympathy.

Williams' use of the epigram is therefore complex. It calls attention as much to the poet who wrote the excerpt as to the message it contains. It also has the tautness of themes and symbolic language that Williams himself uses. It gives a foretaste of the major ideas in *Streetcar,* and their method of construction. It may have been one source of inspiration for the play.

INTRODUCTION

If the epigram to the play is a private and complex introduction, the essay Williams wrote for the New York *Times* drama section on November 30, 1947, four days before the play's New York opening, is a public and fairly straightforward one. In it Williams describes the bad effects of his sudden success with *The Glass Menagerie,* and how he was able to release his creativity again for *A Streetcar Named Desire.*

Williams had been catapulted from a life of struggle to one of comfort and security, and found he could no longer trust his former friends. He felt that his world was becoming increasingly false. Only after another of a succession of eye operations was he again able to experience the sincerity of the old friends he had turned away in the early stages of his success. Williams says that *Streetcar* is his triumph over the artist's impulse to allow security to destroy creativity. By implication, the power of security to corrupt and enslave is a major theme in the play.

It is ironic that Williams should feel the need to apologize for his second smash hit in a row, but he is doing more than that — he is moralizing. He quotes William Saroyan in saying that purity of heart is the only good that man can aim at. Again by implication, *Streetcar* deals with moral issues, the most deadly being the choice not to be human, but to succumb to security.

SCENE 1

Summary

Blanche DuBois arrives at the Elysian' Fields in New Orleans one day in May, looking out of place in her refined white suit with gloves and hat. She stands in front of the lower-class, two-room flat where her sister Stella lives. The sisters talk about Stella's husband Stanley, an ex-Master Sergeant in the Army Engineers, and about the living arrangements for Blanche's visit. Then Blanche tells Stella that the family homestead, called Belle Reve, has been lost. When Stanley returns, and while he boisterously sets up a poker match with Steve and Mitch, he meets Blanche and begins to judge her.

Commentary

In the first scene Williams establishes the setting and major characters in the play. Stanley and Mitch, the primary male characters, are the first to enter. Stella and Blanche are clearly shown to be different in class and background from the rest of the characters in this part of New Orleans. The joke about the meat that Stanley tosses to Stella is underscored by the colored woman's prolonged laughter. It represents the carnal aspect of the relationship between Stanley and Stella and, by inference, the coming child who will be born before the play's end. Right from the play's start, Williams is drawing a close connection between sexuality and love.

Blanche's arrival contrasts with the robust action that precedes it. She is tentative and somewhat bewildered by her sister's surroundings. Eunice Hubbell, the Kowalskis' landlord lets her in and asks about Belle Reve, Blanche and Stella's ancestral home. Belle Reve is established here as another symbolic place we can contrast to the Elysian Fields.

Symbols abound in the directions to the Elysian Fields. The two streetcars to be taken are called Desire and Cemeteries, names which correspond to life and death. The Elysian Fields of Greek mythology was the place to which warrior heroes travelled after death. All of these ideas are twisted in the Streetcar's action: the Elysian Fields of the play, for example, is a place similar to Hell rather than a blessed and happy place for Blanche; the heroes there are not very heroic and certainly not dead. Williams here uses irony along with symbolism to break the patterns that exist in the mind of the audience.

In the stage direction, Stanley's entrance is given a great deal of emphasis. He is a "gaudy seed-bearer," a "richly feathered male bird," in sharp contrast to his sister-in-law who is described as being like "a moth." His picture, taken while he was in his army uniform, is used to introduce him to Blanche before they meet. When they do meet, he immediately shows that he is crude (when he takes off his shirt), vulgar (when he inquires whether Stella, who is in the bathroom, has fallen in the commode), and ruthlessly prying (when he asks about Blanche's dead husband). Yet he accepts the fact that she will be staying in his flat.

Stanley is given polka music as a kind of *leit motif* (that is, particular music to be played when the audience is to be reminded about a character, in this case about Stanley and his cruelty. Another example of a *leit motif* is the music of the Blue Piano, which is used to symbolize the particular locale of the Elysian Fields).

The power of Belle Reve as a symbol is brought out in the way that Blanche atones for her guilt she feels in losing the place. She lashes out at her sister for leaving the homestead and forcing Blanche to deal with the dying family members and the monstrous debt. The name of the place means "beautiful dream" in French and might be the *real* Elysian Fields of the DuBois family. Its loss means a kind of expulsion from

Paradise. Blanche, it seems, is accustomed to dealing with the horrors of death close up. It is the horror of being alone without money or security that brings her to her sister's flat. She has nowhere else to go, but all she can do is complain about the living conditions which she and her sister must now endure.

From the start Blanche is evasive about some aspects of her past, and lies about others. The only point at which she tells the truth of it is when she tells about losing Belle Reve. She evades telling Eunice about that, and Stanley about Allan who had been her husband. She lies to Stella about her leave of absence from teaching and about the real reason for her arrival. In these lies she is later ensnared because the truth is discovered.

The tone of the first scene is one of irony. The low-class neighborhood has an easy charm in spite of the vulgarity and violence that permeate it. The sister who comes for charity does nothing but carp and snipe about what she receives. Stanley, whose crude manners are immediately demonstrated, assents at once to Blanche's staying in his tiny flat despite the inconvenience this will cause he and Stella. Blanche claims to have trouble with a nervous condition (this is substantiated right away by her reaction to the two screechings of the cat). Yet she has no mercy when criticizing her sister for leaving the family deaths and debts in her charge so that she can make love with her crude, lower-class husband. Stanley's later cruelties must be measured against Blanche's now.

SCENE 2

Summary

The next evening, just before going out to a restaurant with Blanche, Stella tells Stanley not to mention her baby and reveals that Belle Reve has been lost. Stanley is upset about the loss because, by Louisiana state law, it was partly his. He suspects that Blanche sold the estate to buy expensive clothes and to live well, and he confronts Blanche to learn how Belle Reve was lost. She shows him the papers, and he tells her Stella is pregnant.

Commentary

Only 24 hours after Blanche's arrival, Stella and Stanley have begun to take sides over her stay. Stella tries to protect her sister against the vulgarity of Stanley's habits by removing her from the home while the poker match is going on. Stanley wants to know just where the family money has gone. He is convinced that Blanche has squandered it. He goes to the extreme of pulling her clothes out of her trunk to demonstrate to Stella where the money probably went — into fine ladies' wear. He does not know that most of the clothing is cheap costumery or gifts.

While Stanley and Stella talk about Blanche, she is in the bath singing. This pattern of Blanche's bathing continues throughout the work. Often the songs she sings escape the bathroom and are heard by the audience; many of these are meaningful, if only to punctuate the talk of others by her implied presence. Bathing may be a symbol for the ritual cleansing of hidden guilt, or merely a means of cooling down and relaxing to soothe her nervous condition.

The almost continuous presence of someone in the bathroom places a focus on that space through most of the play. The room is a place of exercising the most basic of physical needs, and by the set-up of the flat, it is more a public than a private vehicle, acting at times like a thoroughfare, at others like a bottleneck. Hence it is a symbol of the lower-class environment that Stella has chosen for herself, a place that is just as Stanley would wish it.

Stanley's announcement to Blanche about Stella's being pregnant is noteworthy for several reasons. First, though Stella wanted to keep the pregnancy a secret from Blanche, Stanley tells her not ten minutes after hearing Stella's wishes. Second, Stanley brings it up to justify his interest in the sale of Belle Reve, since the money is really the unborn baby's as well as his and Stella's. Third, music from the Blue Piano swells up at the announcement, as if the locale itself is celebrating its triumph over the DuBois family. Fourth, Blanche seems for the moment to be reconciled to Stanley's brutality because of her joy about mixing the DuBois blood and carrying on the line. The expected baby is clearly a symbol of the mingling of two classes, and of the necessary physical acceptance of Stanley's type of person for the continuation of the traditions in whatever form they are to survive.

The trunk that Blanche has brought, and its contents, become symbols through the prying hands and eyes of Stanley, who wants to get to the bottom of the Belle Reve mystery.

Important in this cache of symbols are: the papers about the liquidation of the estate; the letters and poems that represent Blanche's lost love; and the rhinestone tiara that will appear again in Scene 10 just before Blanche's rape. In that scene it will become clear that the rape is just an extension of the intrusion Stanley makes on Blanche's private memories and belongings in Scene 1.

The letters are perplexing as symbols. After Stanley has touched them, Blanche thinks that they are defiled and should be burned. When Stanley presses her to say why, Blanche backs off, evading him. She does say that the boy who wrote the poems was vulnerable, while she is not. Yet, through the packet of poems, she is clearly vulnerable. She does not ever come to know herself. Later her vulnerability will become very clear.

Blanche unashamedly flirts with Stanley when she emerges from the bath. She asks him to button her dress and then to share his cigarette with her. She even fishes for his compliments, which he will not give. Having failed by other means to gain his attention, Blanche sprays him with her atomizer. After Blanche learns that Stella will have his baby, she even tells her sister that she flirted with him as part of her campaign to earn his good will while she explained about the loss of Belle Reve.

This is not an isolated attempt by Blanche to tease men, and it shows Blanche's difficulty, for all her attractiveness, in dealing with mature men. When she says that "a woman's charm is fifty percent illusion" she is admitting that she tells lies, but she does not go on to say she has trouble knowing what the truth is. Flirting is not communicating, except on the most banal level, any more than violence is. Williams seems to be criticising both flirtation and violence as false and dehumanizing.

Stanley's inability to perceive the truth for himself is a symptom of a general disease in modern man. In order to find the truth about the papers that Blanche gives him, he must consult a lawyer. In order to find the value of the wardrobe Blanche brings, he must have it examined by an appraiser. In order to discover what Blanche did in Laurel, he must ask other people in his company. He does not know things in and of themselves, except as they relate to male and female, threatening or non-threatening, vulnerable or invulnerable. Because he does not have the means to judge for himself, he is cruel and narrow in his actions. He does not look past conditions to find causes. And he cannot find the flexibility for change or charity. He will incite tragedy when the right mix of conditions presents itself.

The red satin robe Blanche wears in this scene will be worn by her again, most memorably in Scene 11 just before she is taken to the asylum. It will be a parallel to the robe that Stanley wore on his wedding night and that he puts on just before he rapes Blanche in Scene 10. Clothing, throughout the play, is significant for what it suggests about the wearer, and so are the colors of the clothing. For example, the red of Blanche's robe suggests carnality, just as the white of her dresses in Scenes 1 and 10 imply purity and vulnerability (For elaboration, see the essay on the play's costumery at the end of this Guide.)

SCENE 3

Summary

While the sisters are out, Stanley and his male friends — Pablo Gonzales, Mitch Mitchell, and Steve Hubbell — play poker. Blanche takes an interest in Mitch when she and Stella return, and she talks with him, the two sharing memories of their pasts. When Blanche turns on a radio, Stanley throws it out of the window in a rage, then turns on Stella and strikes her. He is restrained by his friends while Stella escapes to the Hubbells' upstairs flat. Even after this abuse, Stella comes down when Stanley yells like an animal. Afterwards Mitch and Blanche smoke cigarettes together on the steps.

Commentary

This scene is one of the most powerful in American drama. Its focus is the poker game. At one time in an earlier draft, this game had been the centre of the play as a whole.

Poker evokes a wealth of themes. It is a supremely male sport, associated with chance, money, luck, skill, the bluff, and minor vices like hard drinking and chain-smoking. The adage that is bad luck to play poker when there are women in the house is not only old and trivial but also true in this case, as Pablo points out. The high tension and concentration are heightened by a long evening of prolonged drinking to produce a potentially explosive situation. In this scene it is not only the return of Stella and Blanche from the evening out that touches off the situation. It is also Mitch's dropping out of the game while he is ahead.

Mitch is attracted to Blanche, whose music on the radio annoys Stanley anyway. While Mitch and Blanche get to know each other in the bedroom, Stanley insistently calls Mitch back into the other room to return to the game. Finally, when Blanche turns up a waltz and begins to dance, Stanley loses all patience. He storms into the room and hurls the radio out the window. This symbolic action, which is done in jealousy over Blanche's taking Mitch from the game and from his controlling power, is only the first in a steady, irrational, and potentially deadly stream from Stanley. As if mad, he strikes Stella when she tries to send everyone home, and would do worse were he not restrained by the other men and thrust under a cold shower. When he comes to his senses, he is immediately sorry.

Poker provides a social context into which Mitch has always fit. Mitch's winning, then withdrawing into Blanche's social sphere — Blanche is Stanley's rival for mastery of the house — is a violation of the code of the game. Here and later in Scene 11, poker is used as a way of providing order and meaning in the face of an external world which is both turbulent and unknown. Poker is not a good substitute for meaningful life, but Stanley cares little about meaning as long as he is Master Sergeant in charge of everyone around him.

The stage direction at the head of this scene extends the symbolism of the color of clothing. The men all wear primary or at least bold colors, showing that they are proud males, strong, youthful, and virile. Their clothing is in stark contrast to, for example Stella's light blue kimono or Blanche's pink brassiere or white skirt. When Blanche slips into her red satin robe, that gesture signifies her ability to compete with the males.

In this scene we see for the first time the colored paper lantern that Blanche has bought in the Chinese shop on Bourbon Street. She asks Mitch to put it over the light bulb; it will remain there until Mitch, by that time disillusioned, takes it off in Scene 9. While the lantern is over the bulb, Mitch and Blanche have a chance at a lasting relationship. Mitch knows instinctively about symbols, and when the relationship is impossible and he wants to see Blanche without the obscuring power of a shade, he takes it off. The shade is the symbol of romance and also of secrets or lies. The pure light is a symbol of realism and truth.

Stanley's violence is directed at the mass media, two of whose instruments he nearly destroys. The small white radio that he throws out the window is only an extension of Blanche's wishes to keep Mitch from the game for her own purposes. The phone that Stanley hurls to the floor is only the instrument that cannot call Stella home. More effective in expressing his feelings are the slap he gives Stella, the animal cries he makes to call her home, and the embraces he gives her as he takes her into his bed. The vision of his taking Stella into the bed is repeated grotesquely in Scene 10 when he rapes Blanche.

One other symbol that has resonance throughout the play is the silver cigarette case that Mitch shows to Blanche twice. It was given him by a girl who knew she was going to die. The inscription is by the poet Browning and implies that the girl loved Mitch and tried to console him after he learned of her imminent death, with the hope that her love might be even better afterwards. The silver case is later paralleled by the silver mirror Blanche used to search her face in Scenes 10 and 11. The case is a symbol of love, and of attempted communication beyond the boundaries of mortality. The mirror is a symbol of a woman's self-love in the face of mortality.

SCENE 4

Summary

The next morning Blanche, who has spent a sleepless night of worry, learns that Stella takes Stanley's behavior philosophically and even admits to enjoying it. As Stella prepares to clean up the mess left by the poker players, Blanche tells her about Shep Huntleigh, a former flame and now an oil millionaire, she attempts to write a telegram to him asking for enough money to buy a shop for her and her sister. But Stella says she has no need to escape from her situation. Blanche is incensed and, not knowing that Stanley has returned to overhear her, tells Stella just how bestial and common she thinks Stanley is. Even still, Stella embraces him when he comes through the door.

Commentary

Stella, as described in the stage direction at the beginning of this scene, is very contented. She is like an eastern idol, yet she holds a comic book. Her house is a thorough mess, with bottles and the residue of the poker night strewn everywhere, and she has experienced the extremes of violence and passion at the hands of her husband, yet she also knows a happiness that makes her sister Blanche lash out at her in self-defense. Stella has the stability and strength of her relationship with Stanley; all Blanche knows is illusions.

One of the most ironic situations in the play occurs when Stanley overhears Blanche tell her sister just what an animal she thinks Stanley is. Stanley pretends not to have heard, and he is very pleased that Stella has not listened to her sister. The embrace they share before the defeated Blanche is, like the coming child, clear proof there is bond between them. The grin that Stanley gives Blanche suggests that he knows he will have final victory in what is now a struggle for emotional survival.

Blanche's diatribe on the ape-like habits of Stanley and his friends shows both the power of her eloquence and her lack of ability to effect any change with it. Her speech is a defense of civilisation, a testament that man is more than a mere savage and has learned to leave his cave of ignorance. She uses the image of a flag that she urges Stella to wave as she goes forward with progress, but Stella chooses the broom with which she will clean up after Stanley. She does not share Blanche's ideals or illusions. Before and after the speech, as if to bracket it and give it emphasis, the audience hears the sound of a train. Symbolically, Stanley comes home covered with grease from helping the mechanics at Fritz's. Then, even though he is filthy, Stella hugs him anyway.

Stella proves here that she has a strong will. She left home to go to work and married Stanley because she saw in him a man who had the drive to rise in the world as it is now. At least she thinks he has a chance. But Blanche also has a strong will. Here, having spent a sleepless night thinking about a kind of violence that she abhors, she rises in defence of ideals that deserve defending. But her ideals cannot match the attained happiness that Stella has found, a happiness that Blanche will never know firsthand, or understand.

SCENE 5

Summary

Blanche begins to write a fantasy letter to Shep Huntleigh, but is interrupted by a family feud between Steve and Eunice. Stanley lets Blanche know he has spoken to a man named Shaw who claims to have known about her when she lived at the Hotel Flamingo in Laurel. Blanche is shaken by the news, especially when Stanley says he will check on the story. Alone with Stella, Blanche is nervous and tells her about rumors that (false, she claims) were spread about her in Laurel. She is very concerned about her advancing age and how she must deceive Mitch about it until he proposes to her. She sees Mitch as a source of rest for her troubled soul and also as a means of getting clear of Stanley and Stella's life — she senses she is no longer welcome. When Stanley calls Stella away to the Four Deuces, Blanche teases a young collector who happens along past the sidewalk, and kisses him unashamedly. Then she turns to greet Mitch as if this never happened.

Commentary

Blanche now shows us evidence of her worsening mental state. We see the most visible signs are in her dealings with and about men. The scene opens with her laughing about a letter she has drafted to Shep Huntleigh — a letter full of lies about what she is doing. She teases Stanley about his astrological sign, inducing him to hurt her with the knowledge that he has turned up some dirt about her background in Laurel.

After the others have all left, and before Mitch arrives to take her out for the evening, she kisses a strange young collector on the mouth. Her range of emotions in this sequence will strain the talents of an excellent actress; Blanche in this scene assumes a great many roles in succession — she is alternately giddy, flirtacious, guilty, insane, and romantic. Whatever integrity she had is escaping her.

The interchange between Blanche and Stanley about astrology is significant. Blanche is a Virgo (as ironical as her name, which means "white"). She associates herself with virginity throughout the play, regardless of the "facts" to the contrary. She even associates herself with the Blessed Virgin before she is taken away in Scene 11. In contrast, Stanley is not an Aries, as Blanche guesses. He is a Capricorn which is the sign of the goat, an ancient symbol for lechery. This clashing of signs foreshadows the rape in Scene 10 when both players conform to their astrological roles. (Note the rape occurs in September which is Virgo's interval; the rape occurs, under the sign of the virgin just when Stella is having her baby.)

Steve and Eunice Hubbell provide perspective on the relationship between Stanley and Stella, for they are even more violent and abusive. They are also more ready to make up afterwards than the Kowalskis. Since the Hubbells own the building, including the Kowalskis' flat, they in a sense govern the setting. Their antics lend a comic atmosphere to the play. But the couple also (in the case of Eunice) lends a hand when it's needed. The impression we gain by their inclusion in the action is that the play's society is violent and sensual by alternations; the Hubbells are probably the extreme case of this. Eunice's threatening to call the police, her accusing Steve of "going up" (that is, cheating on her) at a local establishment, and the Hubbells' epic struggling in their own flat above the Kowalskis, are all in contrast to Eunice's helpfulness to Blanche in the opening and closing scenes of the play. Also, it is Eunice who gives refuge to Stella after the violence of the poker night and who gives Stella the baby after Blanche goes away forever. So, as in the case of Eunice (whose name in Greek means "good victory"), the mingling of a violent and passionate lifestyle with human concern and kindness becomes a principle of society that everyone within it understands.

When Blanche tells Stella about her reputation (but not the details) in Laurel after losing Belle Reve, Blanche describes herself as "never . . . bad or self-sufficient enough." She relates her vulnerability to the subdued color of clothing she wears and to the paper lantern that she has placed over the light. In doing this she has pointed out the symbolic framework in which she has half-consciously enveloped herself. As a person with some literary background, she has become part of a complex fiction of her own making. The extent of her symbol-making is difficult to measure, but it is clear that she uses symbols very consciously and that she would like to see the world as orderly, as if it were a fine book come to life.

When Blanche discusses her relationship with Mitch, it is revealing because of her total lack of feeling for him as a person. She does not seek love from him, only security. She wants rest. When she says she would like to make Mitch want her, she has no sexual designs whatever. She wants marriage and what that will bring — stability and peace. She admits that she has not "put out" and that she must keep Mitch off balance until he is caught. This is serious business for her, a test she does not think she can afford to fail at her age.

The entire sequence with the young collector emphasizes the yearning in Blanche that Mitch can never satisfy. Because no one but Blanche is at home during this sequence, it could almost be another one of her fantasies, except that this one has come to life. No mention is made of the kiss she gives to the boy later in the play. The sequence establishes that even now Blanche is the same woman who once married a seventeen-year-old boy and also may have seduced a male student from her school in Laurel. Blanche's behavior takes no skill; its only reward is in the magic she senses in the innocence the boy represents. She acknowledges that the event is in one of those time windows that serves as a "little piece of eternity." Perhaps she thinks of him as a connection to the dead boy she married before learning the truth about his homosexuality; perhaps also she subconsciously relates him to the Browning quotation on Mitch's cigarette case.

SCENE 6

Summary

Mitch and Blanche return to the flat in the early hours of the morning. Neither seems to have had a good time out. Blanche is careful to keep the lights down. She speaks French to Mitch, and plies him with liquor. Mitch in this scene personifies sweating, strength and weight; when he lifts her up, she pretends to have old fashioned ideals. When the conversation turns to Stanley, Blanche confesses that she thinks Stanley is her destroyer. Mitch asks Blanche her age because his ailing mother wants to know, but Blanche turns the conversation to his filial love and to her unfortunate discovery of her former husband's homosexuality, and his subsequent suicide. Her account of lost love triggers in Mitch an awareness of both their needs. He implies they might need each other, and in this she sees the answer to her hopes.

Commentary

The plaster statuette of Mae West that Mitch carries upside down is a subtle stage symbol of the sexuality that Mitch would like to control. He has been confused by Blanche, and both of them are miserable. Williams' strategy in this scene is to make the audience uneasy and a little embarrassed, perhaps even slightly bored with the lifeless conversation as Mitch and Blanche first try to communicate. This is so that when Blanche does suddenly open up — in a rare moment of candor — her moving story of Allan completely captivates the audience as well as her guest.

The story of Moon Lake Casino is one of the most memorable vignettes in the play. This is surprising because the players are never seen except through Blanche's rendition of what occurred. Mitch has just told Blanche about his love for his mother, and in return Blanche tells him about *her* only love — Allan. She tells about their love, his sensitivity, their elopement, her discovery that he is a homosexual, their attempt not to face the fact, her abrupt confession of her disgust with him on the dance floor at the Moon Lake Casino, and his horrible suicide by the lakeside there. The Varsouviana is the dance they had been dancing when she told the boy how she really felt. This dance represents both their love and her betrayal of it, her guilt and the barrier to happiness his homosexuality represented. Hidden in the memory of her story is the shadowy figure of the older man who was Allan's friend.

Mathematically, this scene is in the very centre of the play, with five scenes before it and five after it. Though the story's events happened many years before, Blanche's relationship with Allan colors everything she thinks about men. It is the central memory in her life. Ironically, the story allows Allan, through Blanche's memory of him, to provide the means of connecting with Mitch, however briefly. Through the deep sympathy that Mitch feels through Blanche's telling of the tale, he draws her close to him, and the two think they may have possibilities.

The story is revealing because of her telling it at all. At the end of the first scene Stanley asks Blanche about her husband, and Blanche is immediately sick. Now, after a few nights out with Mitch, she goes right to the centre of the experience, revealing her own implication in, and guilt over, the suicide. She reveals also her own shame and outrage over the abnormality

Allan indulged in. She does not seem to plan this as a part of her strategy; rather, it evolves from the conversation, from Blanche's asking him whether he will feel lonely after his mother dies. Their loneliness, together with the fact of the death of a loved one, brings them together.

Blanche herself might benefit from the kind of devotion that Mitch gives to his mother; she may also have sensed Mitch's concern for the loneliness he will feel after his mother's death. But the intruding stage sounds used to accompany her tale seem to come more from within her mind that outside it, indicating that she is reliving it vividly again, as it actually happened. She does not seem to be acting, and her surrender to the moment, when she has let down all her defences, allows her a temporary victory over her facade.

SCENE 7

Summary

Stanley finds Stella preparing a party for Blanche's birthday and tells her with sadistic pride about Blanche's sordid background in Laurel, about her losing her position as a teacher because of her affair with a seventeen-year-old boy, and about her being encouraged to leave town. Stella's reply is that she does not believe the story. She tells Stanley about Blanche's unfortunate marriage, but he is not interested in Blanche's distant past. In fact, he tells Stella not to expect Mitch for the party since he told him everything he had learned about her sister. Now Mitch will not consider marrying Blanche, and Stanley has bought Blanche a bus ticket out of town for Tuesday.

Commentary

In mid-September, under the sign of Virgo, Stella arranges a birthday party for Blanche. Though it should be festive, it starts Blanche's final undoing. Throughout the play Blanche is fearful of becoming old without the reward of security in marriage. The birthday symbolizes the relentlessness of time. In the cake Blanche sees the blue of the expected baby's eyes and, by inference, possibly also the blue in her Allan's eyes. The emptiness of the occasion is compounded by Mitch's absence and by Stanley's cruel gift of a one-way bus ticket back to

Laurel. While Stella has worked to make Blanche's birthday happy, Stanley has worked to cut her off from all future happiness and will later cut her off from all sanity.

Stanley has setout to destroy Blanche, but his motives are not entirely clear. He has already bought the ticket before the party when he confronts Stella with what he has discovered about her sister's reputation. Blanche cannot resist making comments about his vulgarity, but he has heard them all before. Stanley may be striking out at her from pride, from a sense of superior advantage, from malice, from jealousy about her attraction to Mitch, or from jealousy over the relationship she has with Stella. He is, as he tells Stella, eager to get back to the times they had before Blanche arrived.

While Stanley tells Stella about Blanche's sordid past in Laurel, Blanche is blind to the impending evil. She is singing in the bathtub. Her songs are about love, and she seems very happy. Stanley resents her singing and her happiness. He dwells on her lies about the Hotel Flamingo and about having a job to go back to. He will not listen to Stella's attempts to explain her sister's behavior. He has made up his mind and will now not change it. Williams has juxtaposed Stanley's intense and directed hatred with the unaware and blithe Blanche. This can remind us (by opposition) of the earlier irony in Scene 4 in which Stanley overhears Blanche's criticisms of him. The reversal is complete when Stanley tells Stella that he has told Mitch everything and that Mitch will not marry her as he had planned. When she emerges from her bath, Blanche at first feels fresh and happy, but immediately she knows something dreadful has happened.

SCENE 8

Summary

Blanche is embarrassed that she has been stood up by Mitch on her birthday, and tries to be pleasant. But she falls into her usual habit of bringing out the crude side of Stanley, who hurls his dishes to the floor and abuses her verbally. Blanche guesses that Mitch has learned about her past. Stanley clumsily tries to make up with Stella. The cake's candles are lighted, but Stanley and Blanche cannot stop fighting. Finally Stanley gives Blanche the bus ticket he bought for her, and

Blanche runs from the room sick. Stella confronts Stanley about his cruelty, even tearing his shirt, but he only recounts with pride how he pulled Stella down from her refined ideas and how she loved it. Stella now feels birth pangs. She asks Stanley to take her to the hospital.

Commentary

After being set up for the disappointment, the audience is ready for a dismal birthday party. Blanche, who does not immediately know what Stanley has told Mitch, expects him to arrive to fill his place at the table. She is uneasy about being stood up since she asked him to come.

Stella is uneasy because she knows Mitch will not come at all. She is angry with Stanley for causing Mitch to change his mind about her sister and begins talking to Stanley as Blanche did, calling him a pig. In response, he hurls his plate to the floor and stalks out. Only after he makes up with Stella does he return to the table. Yet even then he persists in giving Blanche the bus ticket in a very cruel way, making her leave the room to be sick.

The scene is ugly throughout and bristles with irony. The phone calls do not break the tension; they add to it. Blanche's call finds Mitch not there. When the phone rings again, the call is from Mac, one of Stanley's bowling buddies, who wants to set up a time to bowl. Even though both sisters are critical of him, Stanley seems to go out of his way to show them he is even more bestial, solvenly, and cruel than they say he is.

The resentment he feels for Blanche and for what she represents is one of the strongest arguments in the play for the values she holds. He is proud that he brought Stella low, and he is even prouder that he will do the same thing to her sister.

Stanley's brutality induces Stella's first pangs of childbirth. Blanche alludes to the child when she considers the candles on her cake, but there has been no sign of labor coming on until now. When Stanley brags about what he did with Stella, it is as if the child itself answers. As before, violence and brutality were followed by reconciliation in the sexual union. Now they are followed by the fruits of that union. The child is Stanley's triumph over the distinctions of class and manners. It will be a child born of dominance and suppression, and the only indication of a next generation in the play.

SCENE 9

Summary

Mitch shows up unshaven at the door of the flat, and Blanche tries to deal with his disillusionment. She shows signs of mental deterioration. Mitch rips the lantern covering off the light so that he can see her as if for the first time. He tells Blanche that at first he did not believe Stanley, but verified the story with his company's supply man and with a merchant named Kiefaber in Laurel. Trapped by her past, Blanche tells about the connection between her husband Allan and her fall from respectability. Mitch dwells on her lies — about her age and ideals — and Blanche spurns a passing blind Mexican woman's entreaty to buy tin funeral flowers. When Mitch admits that he will not marry her because she is not clean enough to be in the same house as his mother, Blanche begins screaming "Fire!" just to get rid of him.

Commentary

Mitch's physical appearance when he arrives at the Kowalski home tells us that he has not taken the news about Blanche's past well. Since she is having trouble keeping her sanity — hearing polka music and reliving her husband's death — the two are in tension from the start. While Mitch wants realism, Blanche wants to keep her illusions. Neither will back down. Mitch's aim in his visit is simple — to possess sexually the woman he no longer wants to marry, and to revenge himself on her body for the time he has already lost during the summer's charade. Blanche's aim is to fend off the realism Mitch personifies.

Mitch has made the error of thinking that Blanche has been holding out on him while the truth is she gave of herself to everyone who came along, at least in Laurel. Mitch has no understanding of women, and for all his claims about realism, he is incapable of seeing or doing anything without direction. When he brutally says that he does not think Blanche is clean enough to be in the same house with his mother, she turns on him with indignation.

There is a good chance that Mitch is now acting on Stanley's instructions. Mitch cannot do anything by himself and

Stanley alluded to Mitch's perhaps still wanting Blanche, but not as a wife. It is made clear in Scene 10 that Mitch reports to Stanley almost immediately after this encounter with Blanche. It is also clear that part of Stanley's aim is to finish himself what he sent Mitch to accomplish. What is left unclear is just how far Stanley has been involved in the affair from the start, and what his motives are. Williams will not allow a very specific analysis of this complex possibility.

The symbols in this scene are few but striking. They are light and fire. The light is Mitch's symbol for what he calls realism but may instead be the light of disillusionment. To Blanche, the lantern cover for the light stands for magic, illusion, and romance. The two symbols work together well enough that both know what taking the lantern off the light means. Fire is another kind of light — when Blanche cries out *Fire!* she effectively puts out the fire of passion that might have proved tragic. By calling out the word, Blanche scares Mitch away, but she has to go to the window and bellow frantically to do so.

An apparent anomaly in the scene is the Mexican woman who sells the tin funeral flowers. She seems to come out of nowhere and then to disappear. Her function is complex. We don't know anything about her character, her thoughts or her feelings, or even the price of her wares. Clearly she is a symbol of death because of what she sells, but she is also more. She appears just after Blanche has told Mitch she never lied in her heart to anyone. The sudden appearance of the woman seems to bring that into question. The tin flowers and crowns she sells are paupers' devotionals. Perhaps there is a connection between Blanche with her type of moral blindness and the Mexican woman with her actual blindness. Williams leaves the symbol to speak for itself.

The death symbols may be significant for a number of things — for Blanche, for her illusions, for the death of her hope of marriage with Mitch, for the thing that died between them, and for the effects of the lies that Blanche has told. The woman uses the word *flores,* or flowers, just as Mitch uses the word *lies* or as Blanche uses the word *fire.* There is some doubt that the woman exists outside Blanche's mind — she may be just another product of her fantasy. Mitch does not seem to hear the woman. The stream of images that comes from the dark corners of Blanche's mind, and bring to mind the story of the Moon Lake Casino, have little effect now.

SCENE 10

Summary

After inspecting herself in it, Blanche breaks a silver mirror just as Stanley returns from the hospital. Blanche has dressed up and pretends to have received a telegram from Shep Huntleigh. Stanley extracts from a drawer the silk pyjamas he wore on his wedding night. Then, as Blanche tries to invent an honorable story regarding her break-up with Mitch and her relationship with Shep Huntleigh, Stanley relentlessly cuts through the tissue of lies she tells. As he corners her, Blanche tries desperately to make her Huntleigh myth come to life by calling him long distance. The stage becomes an extension of Blanche's tormented soul. In dumb show, outside the window, a sordid scene appears of a prostitute rolling a drunk. When Blanche tries the phone again, Stanley emerges from the bathroom in his pyjamas. He easily fends off the broken bottle which she uses to defend herself and carries her into the bed.

Commentary

A number of times in the play, Stanley mockingly calls Blanche a queen.

When he first went through her trunk he latched onto her rhinestone tiara, thinking it was expensive. Now Blanche wears the crown along with her white satin evening gown. The cue for Stanley's entrance is Blanche's breaking her silver mirror face down on her dresser. She did not like what she saw in the mirror — perhaps it was age, sorrow, and fear. The mirror is the symbol of introspection as well as the woman's pride, and it can reveal guilt and despair as well as wrinkles and bags about the eyes. When she cracks the mirror she is denying what she sees, whatever it is, and in that denial we can detect a symptom of madness.

Coming at the beginning of the scene, it is a parallel for the breaking of her inner most privacy by Stanley, who successfully denies her the right to her illusions. He will not let her fall back on a fictional wire from Shep Huntleigh, or console herself with a lie about Mitch's returning with flowers and an apology.

Stanley himself has a rare moment of insight when he sees a relation between Blanche's millionaire Huntleigh and his baby — the one is fantasy, the other miraculous reality.

As if to draw the two together, Stanley, as if he were performing a ritual, takes out his pyjama top, which he claims he will take off and wave like a flag when the phone rings with the news of his child's birth. The image of the flag here harks back to the flag image used by Blanche in her earlier speech about Stanley's brutality. Then Blanche urged Stella to wave the flag of progress and civilization. Here Stanley's use of the flag symbol reverses the former meaning, for in the pyjama coat that is his flag, he broke down the civilized Stella and made her his wife. But here the symbol is carried even further — after a heated exchange of words with Blanche, Stanley puts the coat on and rapes her in it. This act parallels the event with Stella.

When it becomes clear to Blanche what Stanley intends for her, she becomes frantic and tries futilely to use the phone. She has visions which include a "dumb show" of a prostitute being attacked by a drunk she has rolled, and another of the Negro Woman from Scene 1 rifling the prostitute's sequined bag. The message she tries to send through Western Union is almost exactly the same as the one she advised Stella to send the morning after the poker night. But this time the desperation is more immediate, for Stanley has emerged from the bathroom to place the phone on the hook. He corners the frantic woman to the swelling music of the Blue Piano.

SCENE 11

Summary

The action opens again weeks later with the men playing poker and the women preparing for Blanche's departure. Stella, who has had her baby, admits that she could not both believe her sister's story and go on living with Stanley. She has made the decision to stay, and sealed her sister's fate. Blanche emerges as a tragic figure still asking about the expected call from Shep Huntleigh. The women have made up a story about Blanche going on a vacation; she envisions a sea vacation and her own death at sea. The doctor and nurse from the asylum arrive to take Blanche away. Right away Blanche realizes that something is wrong. While all the others watch tensely for the final outcome, Blanche takes the doctor's arm and goes out with him. To calm Stella, Eunice gives her the new baby to hold, and the men proceed to finish their poker game.

Commentary

Scene 11 and Scene 1 are complementary. Blanche arrives in Scene 1 to be oriented by Eunice and departs in Scene 11 assisted by Eunice. As a reminder of the critical poker night of Scene 3, the men play while the women prepare for Blanche's departure. Blanche is now acting much like a queen, but her regal composure is shown to be broken. Some of the passages indicate that her mind is almost wholly gone. Like many stage mad women, she is wise in her madness and foolish with her wits. She commands Stella and Eunice as if they are her ladies-in-waiting; they serve her out of respect and pity, and perhaps also guilt because they know where she is going and what it means.

Stella and Eunice discuss the decision in a few lines. It is clear that Stella has had her sister committed. It is also clear that Stella made that decision because she felt if she believed Blanche's story (presumably about Stanley raping her), she could not go on living with her husband. It is not clear whether she asked Stanley about the accusation or that he volunteered any information about the incident. There is a strong suggestion that Stella feels so tied to Stanley that she simply made a pragmatic decision, one that was unrelated to the truth of what happened. Her possible motives — jealousy, the new baby, fear of the unknown, a sense of triumph in the final defeat of her older sister, and her just being tired of company — are not explored in the play. Eunice's consolation, "Life has got to go on," is not as satisfying as the symbol of that life — the baby — whom Eunice gives Stella just after the doctor has led Blanche away.

This final scene does not just repeat symbols like the mirror, the poker game, and the red satin robe. It also adds and develops new ones. The sea horse clasp that Blanche wishes to wear is part of an image that continues in her vision of her own death at sea. In the vision is packed a great many sumbols from everywhere in the work — the grapes from the beginning of this scene, the young ship's doctor from the succession of young men whom Blanche has known, the clean white sack from the many white costumes that she wears (here clearly a death symbol), the blue of Allan's eyes and her wish for a blue-eyed baby for Stella. At the mention of Allan's eyes, the doctor and nurse from the state institution appear. Clearly Blanche's insanity is partial, but her experience in the Elysian Fields has prepared her for a kind of death-like existence where she will have continual observation and care.

Setting

The world of *A Streetcar Named Desire* is post-World War II America. It was a time when ex-soldiers like Stanley Kowalski and his friends from the 242nd Engineers were settling back into civilian life after the years of conflict. Opportunities were available for hard-driving men, especially those who could carve out new territories in sales, and for well-trained technicians and machinists like Mitch whose ambitions were modest and whose expectations were ordinary. The melting-pot America of post-war New Orleans was well-suited to an easy mix of races and ethnic types, at least in the lower classes of society. Ironically, life in a country tired of fighting a war became elemental, even brutal, as other conflicts — commercial, familial, and sexual — emerged from beneath the peaceful surfaces.

This war radically transformed America — much more than did World War I. Armies no longer were formed along the time-honored lines of territories with a local person in the lead; instead, the entire structure down to the platoon level was geared to mixing men of regions, ethnic types, and classes. Industry had been so involved in the war effort that afterwards it had to start again virtually from scratch. It also had to struggle to absorb the vast labor force that poured out of the services, and to invent the formulas for doing business that today are clichés. Norman Mailer's novel *The Naked and the Dead* (1948) told the story of how men, thrown together in this new way, interacted during the war. One year earlier Williams' play had shown what came afterwards. It is a kind of continuation of Mailer's grim story about a new emerging America, a country in which brute force and street wisdom were winning out over the old ideals of culture.

But Williams' New Orleans setting showed another conflict being overlaid on the melting-pot conflict. This was the clash between the dying Southern aristocracy and the laboring class. The roots of the latter extended back to a time of history called the Reconstruction (1865-1877). That era was the cruel adjustment period for the South after it lost the Civil War. Many members of the old Southern aristocracy were forced to sell their plantations to keep up their displays of refinement; they had no way of dealing with the new economy except by turning their backs on their traditions. Southern women were particularly hard-hit since they had little place in the economy and since the traditional way for a well-bred Southern woman to maintain her position — to marry a wealthy landowner — was becoming increasingly difficult.

One aspect of the setting of *A Streetcar Named Desire* that is hard to understand in the 1980s is its social and moral code with respect to women. Although women were in the labor force during the war that situation was considered, by everyone including working women, as temporary. According to the code, women were to remain at home with the family while the husband worked. Every woman needed to attach herself to a provider-male while she was still young enough and attractive enough to get one. Also, according to the code, she must come to marriage as a virgin, with an unblemished reputation, and must be pliable in marriage and suffer whatever the bread-winner husband wished, within rather broad boundaries. Since she could not work without breaking her society's taboos (though there were isolated exceptions) and since she had to observe special rules of sexual conduct, she was at the mercy of a male-dominated world. Her position offered her the privilege of secret dreams and illusions, but only if in public she conformed to social norms. In approaching a play like *Streetcar,* one must accept this unwritten code as a given.

The moral code was even more severe regarding both madness and homosexuality. Blanche DuBois has not only a bad reputation from her time in Laurel. She also has a tragic connection to a homosexual and a marked tendency toward insanity. With all that, she is tainted from the start. At the time of its first performance, *Streetcar* was a daring play that dealt frankly with major social taboos. Less provocative, but still shocking in the 1940's, were things like: the dress and manner of Stanley Kowalski and Blanche; Stanley's verbal and physical violence, and especially his rape of Blanche; the ethnic types chosen for portrayal; the embarrassing and prolonged fantasies of Blanche; and the final appearance of the asylum personnel. Then and for many years afterwards, Williams was considered by many moral critics to be a decadent and even depraved playwright, yet the best of his plays still hold the stage today.

Structure

Williams used a number of structural devices in creating *Streetcar*. The most obvious unifying elements are the stage setting, which leaves the two rooms and the street open to the audience throughout, and the character Blanche, who appears as the central figure in each scene.

Williams uses time to group scenes together. The first four scenes (which are often followed by an intermission in the theatre) involve the first two days of Blanche's arrival. Scenes 5 and 6 develop the relationship between Blanche and Mitch while Stanley pries into her background. Scenes 7 through 10 focus on Blanche's birthday party and rape, which occur hours apart. Scene 11, in which Blanche is committed to an asylum, is a kind of wrap-up.

Seen from one perspective, the play is structured around the struggle between Blanche and Stanley for mastery of the house. Stanley wins in nearly every contest, and while this struggle is a unifying element and central to the action, it is not exclusive.

For example, from another perspective, Blanche's illusions are struggling for survival against the realities of her past. In this framework, Stanley is only one agent in Blanche's story. Others are Mitch, Allan, and Stella. In each of the four parts of the play, Blanche's sanity is tested and is increasingly found wanting. In the end, of course, she has gone mad. Williams makes the actions in both plot strands lead to a climax (in Stanley's case, a sexual one) in the rape of Blanche in Scene 10.

A third strand of the story would center on Blanche's attempt to form lasting relationships with Stella and Mitch. In this case, Stella begins by defending Blanche in spite of several things Blanche does and says to her, but in the end must agree to have her committed to the asylum. Within this action is the relationship with Mitch, which follows a familiar pattern of a rising relationship which fails and is cut off by both parties.

In fact, all three of these perspectives are allowable in the play, and each is supported by its own pattern of imagery and symbolism.

Themes

A theme is a word, like *death, alienation* or *love,* which, through its association with other themes and symbols, shows us the basis for the ideas within a literary work. A theme can be stated or implied. In some works only one theme is dealt with; in others — the greatest literature — so many themes are dealt with in such a complex and lifelike way that the work contains the conflicts and tensions of life itself. Williams uses a vast network of themes to give his work the impression of real life. He succeeds even though he uses stock characters and stock, though sensational, situations. He is especially skillful at weaving together conflicting themes and at relating those to symbols through the language of his characters. Note that many of his characters think in abstract, or thematic, ways.

Two apparently conflicting themes, love and violence, define the relationship between Stella and Stanley. Blanche cannot tolerate the mingling of a bond she sees as romantic with the brute animal force that Stanley represents. She is caught between the conflicting themes of appearance (what she would like to be) and reality (what she was for a brief time in Laurel before having to take refuge in her sister's home). The vitality in Williams' drama often results from the irony of a person's having to deal with apparent contradictions (see below).

One very clear use of themes in the play is associated with a major symbol — the title's symbol of the streetcar name Desire. In fact there actually was such a streetcar in New Orleans, but the theme of desire is so dominant in the play that the other themes cluster around it as if it were a character in itself. Stella speaks wistfully about Stanley in terms of her physical desire for him. Blanche repeatedly alludes to her own desires. Stanley and Mitch desire in different ways at different times. So desire, which is clearly related to our driving instinct for life, is also related to sex, illusion, lust, loneliness, and a host of other themes. Often overlooked in Blanche's itinerary to Elysian Fields is the necessary transfer from the streetcar named Desire to the one named Cemeteries. Blanche knows this progression from her own history — Allan, the family deaths and Mr. Graves' actions — and repeats the thematic progression at the end of the play through her victimization — her rape by Stanley and commitment to the asylum. Desire intersects, then, the themes of death and madness, and — through Blanche's fantasies only — the themes of rest and peace.

Themes can be musical or even physical as well as abstract. The various musical themes in the play act as *motifs* do in operas. They signal the similarity of actions or interactions of the characters. For example, the polka is associated with Stanley, who is Polish. The Varsouviana is a memory theme associated with Blanche's tragic time with Allan. The music of the Blue Piano punctuates the play, and almost becomes the spirit of the house. The screeching of the cat or the sound of the trains also work in this way.

When objects on the stage are used repeatedly, not symbolically but for their own sakes on the stage, they may carry the force of a theme. An example of such an object used as a theme is the deck of cards for playing poker. It symbolizes nothing, but is used repeatedly and defines the space on the stage. Drinks and cigarettes have a similar thematic purpose. The theme of drink is related to the theme of nerves in Blanche, and the theme of cigarettes intersects the theme of communication, positively when used with Blanche and Mitch, negatively when used with Blanche and Stanley.

The theme of carnality, associated almost mythically with New Orleans, is present from the first toss of the meat package by Stanley to the rape of Blanche. It is related to the complex central theme of desire. Colors, which can be thematic also, are related to this theme — particularly red, a dominant color in the play.

One theme in *Streetcar* that critics have surprisingly overlooked is the theme of literary allusion, especially in Blanche's speech. When she compares the Elysian Fields to Edgar Allan Poe's "ghoul-haunted woodland of Weir," the audience is reminded of her profession as an English teacher, of her propensity for imaginative and even shocking analogies, and of her morbidity. Of all the characters in the play, she is the most adept at marshalling the English language to express herself and, tragically, the least capable of using it to tell the truth.

Language

When *A Streetcar Named Desire* was first performed, its language was thought to be shocking even in a world made tough through the war experience. The vulgarity extended beyond the vocabulary to the ideas the play presented. The frank attitude towards sex projected in Stella's rhapsodies, the off-color jokes told by both Steve and Blanche, the emphasis on the bathroom by Stanley, and the general atmosphere of jungle antagonism, all brought (and still brings) the moralists forward, in no small part because the champion of the moral causes in the play is Blanche — and she is fallen.

Though the guardian of language, she is blemished and so cannot continue to hold her authority. While Blanche's language is correct, Blanche herself is corrupt. And her corruption goes beyond the superficial kind denoted by her having dwelt at the Hotel Flamingo. She is subject to such lack of judgement (remember the seventeen-year-old male student, and the collector, and probably others) and to such flights of fantasy (her dreams of Huntleigh) that what she says must be weighed very carefully. For all their crudity, Mitch and Stanley speak a language that makes perfect sense. They have no intellectual comprehension; they function at a normal emotional level. Yet when Mitch talks about the love relationship between Stanley and Stella or about needing to see Blanche in the light, he speaks the truth. His truth is not profound, as Blanche would wish it, but neither is it based on the premise that charm is half illusion. Like Stanley, Mitch is a man of very few words, and his words count.

Stage language, always an approximation of the living language, is here a symptom of a society's inability to communicate. The violence erupts mainly because of the failure of language and the almost desperate need to compensate for that failure. Violence is seen as a type of substitute language, just as for Mitch symbols work better than words. Mitch resorts to the symbol of light to express his desire to see — really *see* — Blanche. Ironically, all substitutes for language are inadequate, and lead to violence and pain.

So *Streetcar* is a play about the failure of language, and the breakdown of civilization that results when people like Blanche, who are meant to be the moral cement between language and reality, turn their backs on their proper role. Blanche, in this context, serves not only as a symbol of the breakdown of language but as a symbol of the larger breakdown of civilization itself.

Symbol

Williams once wrote that "Art is made out of symbols the way your body is made out of vital tissue." A play for him was a living organism, and the components of it were symbols. A living symbol is an object, a sensory experience, an action, or an idea that stands for something else when the other thing cannot be exactly defined. Poetry tends to be a kind of symbolic language, and in Williams symbols tend to have even more communicating power than language. *Streetcar* contains a symbol in its title; its staging is symbolic; many objects on the stage are symbols; the lighting, music, action, and even the characters have symbolic overtones. But what makes these symbols work together is how they relate with each other. Like the analogy to the body that Williams made, the living symbols are the tissue for the larger organism, which is also alive on account of them.

Symbols help bring together the major themes of the work. For example, the small white radio that Stanley hurls from the window on poker night, the colored comic Stalla reads after her night of violence and love, the telephone Blanche grabs repeatedly but which Stanley puts decisively down on the hook before the rape, the films and newspaper, all form the media in the world of the play. As media they are supposed to communicate or to hold society together. Instead they serve to communicate the often violent feelings of the user. They symbolize the modern world (phones with dials!), but only its anguish and brutality. Western Union cannot help Blanche to escape, and it even seems to be a barrier rather than a means to reach Shep Huntleigh.

Among the other symbolic patterns we see are costumery (the white party dress in Scene 1, the white satin dress in Scene 10, the red robe, and the blue dress in Scene 11 all have symbolic value for Blanche the victim), music (polka, Varsouviana, Blue Piano music, radio music, and Blanche's singing in the bathtub, symbolize her progress towards madness), and light (the bulbs, the Chinese lantern and the verbal image of the searchlight are all associated with the opposing themes of appearance and reality). These elements are so much a part of the texture of the play and so numerous and powerful that larger-than-normal patterns of symbolism are suggested.

Because the characters are "types" (as admitted by Stella, for example), they are representative or symbolic of whole classes of people. Blanche and Stanley are drawn as individuals, but as individuals who are representative of others like them. Not a small group in New Orleans but the vast population of America seems to be in our view in the sensual, brutal environment of the play.

Further, Williams is not judgmental about the outcome. The complexity of Blanche works against a simple decision for or against her. She gets much more than she deserves by way of punishment for her failings. Yet she is not the martyr she would like to be. Insanity is an ambivalent tragic ending for her. It is not death, but might even be worse because of the prolonging of her suffering and the pain of confinement. So Blanche is an ambivalent heroine who stands for many of the values society holds dear but is unable to stand for any real worth because of her past. While she is being dressed for her final departure in Scene 11, she compares herself to the Madonna. Yet she has been raped by Stanley and she has told about it. Throughout the play she is associated with red and white, the colors of pure blood and absolute purity in traditional literature. But in her case these mean, among other things, her crimson past (and sacrificial rape) and her fatal vulnerability.

Irony

Williams is a master of irony, which he uses in all its forms in the play. He seems to take special delight in shocking ironies, sharp reversals of expectations, and the ironies that could lead to tragedy. Irony is the tension between our expectations and the truths that prove them false when they occur together.

For example, it is ironic that Stanley overhears Blanche tear him apart verbally to his wife; the irony is stronger not just because he keeps his eavesdropping secret but also because Stella embraces him even more warmly after her sister has run him down than she might have beforehand. This kind of irony of situation is supported by other forms of irony in the play — verbal irony and irony of character, for example. The overall effect is to make the world on the stage appear like a vicious trap, one designed to snare nearly everyone who approaches it.

Blanche is the most ironic character, for she is unwittingly at war with herself. She wants a man of refinement, but goes after Mitch. She teases Mitch, then fends him off. She moves in on Stella but then does nothing but complain about her sister's lifestyle. Her illusions are far from reality, and her past is in stark contrast to the values she espouses in the present. Having lost her family estate, she tries to convince Stella to give up her happiness. While her sister is in childbirth Stanley first terrorizes, then rapes her. In short, the character of Blanche is built on the device of irony. She is justly considered to be complex by most critics because of the ironies in her makeup and in her history.

The irony that Stella has found love in an environment of pain does not escape Blanche. That Stella continues to treat Blanche well even after Blanche has hurled abuse at her and her husband is not surprising. After all, Stella puts up with this same type of abuse from Stanley without flinching. What is ironic is Stella's agreeing to commit Blanche to an asylum at the very time Blanche is telling the truth. She agrees to it because she cannot deal with this particular truth about being raped. Blanche's credibility is so damaged by the time of the rape that she is most suspect when she most needs to have someone believe her. She is committed even though she cannot physically harm anyone, while Stanley, whose blind passion can and does harm people, sits in triumph at the end.

Selected Criticisms

The intention of providing these excerpts from a variety of sources is not to endorse what they say but to provide a range of views you can react to or think about. The experience of the play — your experience and your reading — should emerge and become clear as you appraise these and other statements about Williams' play.

Tennessee Williams brings to the stage a distinctly Southern sensibility — a penchant for neo-Lawrencian metaphysics and lyricism, a fascination with grotesquerie, and a fondness for characters incapable of dealing with reality.

Robert F. Kiernan

. . . aspiration, sensitivity, departure from the norm are battered, bruised, and disgraced.

Harold Clurman

While Williams appears to be primarily concerned with sexuality in *Streetcar,* his symbolic depiction of desire transcends merely sexual passion, to include existence itself as its ultimate referent.

Leonard Quirino

Blanche has no illusion about her illusions.

Benjamin Nelson

The word *victim* comes easily when one begins to talk about the characters in Williams' plays, for the rape of Blanche and her subsequent insanity hangs like a banner over Williams' work, proclaiming him the spokesman for the defeated, the frustrated, the beaten.

Gerald Weales

Stanley Kowalski . . . scorns the substance and the surface of clean, properly spoken, middle-class American success, scorns the pride that comes with family lineage. Himself proud only of his greasy, dirty proletarian work and appearance and speech, his whole bearing a defiance of the usual accoutrements of success, he systematically sets out to destroy the barely flickering spark of family pride, perhaps the only success she has ever known, which sustains Blanche DuBois, his sister-in-law.

Morris Freedman

If classical tragedy's completeness, infiniteness, was its insistence on marking for certain destruction the man in the middle, the man who was neither flawless nor hopelessly flawed, *Streetcar's* is its depiction of life's workings as inexplicable, ultimately, in terms of fate or chance exclusively, indeed, as seemingly simultaneously inevitable and incidental.

Bert Cardullo

A Streetcar Named Desire begins where a tragedy has already ended. Its own action transposes the elements of tragedy into ironies, at the expense of the woman whose punishment takes her through a version of the tragic in which no real purpose or perception is possible.

Britton J. Harwood

Blanche's sister, Stella, deals with reality in a basically healthy way. . . . Stella ignores the needs of others and eventually adopts her own illusion. Life with Stanley — sex with Stanley — is her highest value.

Jeanne M. McGlinn

Stanley and Blanche are worthy opponents using different techniques and weapons. Blanche cannot triumph, for the world belongs to the Stanleys, and he must eliminate her if his own values are not to be threatened.

Allan Lewis

Williams' women — Blanche, Maggie the Cat, Alma in *Summer and Smoke,* Baby Doll — they all cry out for defilement, and most of them get it.

John Osborne

Williams is one of the most expert dramatists of this century and his plays keep an audience enthralled because of their skillful construction and the liberal amounts of sex, bawdry, and violence they contain.

Willard Tharp

Blanche herself probably remains Williams' most notable creation. It is because she is such an amalgam of contradictions and because all the barbs are directed at us through her alone that the comic-pathetic note is sounded so frequently through the play.

J. L. Styan

Snatching the eternal out of the desperately fleeting is the great magic trick of human existence.

Tennessee Williams

The tragedy of individual persons, which began in the struggles of the aspiring mind, ends as the fierce animal struggle and relapse: in the single act of sex, where there is a communication in which mind has tragically failed; an act of life and death, in the same rhythms, the tense and cruel struggle consummated at last in relapse. The end of the sex . . . is death.

Raymond Williams

Tennessee Williams' Women: Illusion and Reality, Sexuality and Love*

The critical labels commonly affixed to the women characters in the plays of Tennessee Williams are deceptively simple. Robert Jones divides the "Early Heroines" into basically two types, the gentlewoman of a genteel but mythical southern way of life and the sensual or natural woman. The gentlewoman cannot understand life in the modern world, and in her resultant alientation she seeks to recapture a way of life, the cavalier Old South, which never really existed. The sensual women are inhabitants of the New South and "seem to have been conceived by their creator, if not as representatives of a sort of salvation, then at least as attractive earth goddesses whose salvation is their own sexuality" ("Tennessee Williams' Early Heroines", p. 211). Jones considers sex as either a means of escape or a sign of liberation, depending on the woman's view of her own sexuality. John von Szeliski also feels the basic dramatic action of Williams' plays is sexual ("Tennessee Williams and the Tragedy of Sensitivity", p. 67). Critics agree on reading Williams' plays as sexual dramas in which the southern gentlewoman and the natural woman represent respectively the spirit and the flesh, though the sexual is the only creative and positive form of behavior. Yet a close reading of Williams' plays reveals a complexity in the women that makes these classifications incomplete.

In seven plays written in a twenty year period, Williams uses essentially the same dramatic situation. A woman is presented at a moment when frustration has led to a crisis. She has only two possible ways of acting: to face reality or to retreat into illusion. The significant question is whether she will face the crisis and choose to live in the real world, free of debilitating illusions and capable of compassion for others. Whatever value sex has for Williams, in some plays sexuality leads to illusion or is at least the result of a very self-centered view of reality. Neither situation is creative, whereas the ability to respond to

*By Jeanne M. McGlinn. From *Tennessee Williams: A Tribute*, edited by Jac Tharpe.

the needs of another human being emerges as a higher value for Williams. The human contact may be either physical or spiritual; what matters is the attempt to love — based on a realistic understanding of both oneself and another. Between 1940 and 1960 Williams moves from the delineation of women who live in illusion and hence are unable to love to the delineation of women who accept the reality of their lives and become concerned and compassionate or at least ready for unselfish love.

In two plays of the forties, *The Glass Menagerie* and *A Streetcar Named Desire*, the women characters all act under the influence of an illusionary view of both themselves and their world and so are unloving. In *The Glass Menagerie*, both Amanda and Laura refuse to face the reality of their lives; Amanda retreats into the past, and Laura retreats into herself. Laura's withdrawal is more deadening than Amanda's, however, because she is completely self-centered. Amanda is at least trying to hold the family together, economically and spiritually. She tries to help Laura lead a normal life, first by sending her to business college then by making "plans and provisions" for a gentleman caller. These efforts for another human being, even though undermined eventually by Amanda's illusions, corroborate Williams' description of Amanda as having "dignity and tragic beauty" (Vol. I, p. 236, *The Theatre of Tennessee Williams)*.

The crisis that led to Amanda's illusion came well before the play began. Her husband's desertion of her and the family was the shock that sent her back into the golden days of her girlhood. Since Amanda cannot face the reality that she was unable to hold her husband's love, she indulges in memories of that one supreme moment of her youth, the day when she might have chosen from seventeen gentlemen callers, all rich and successful and caring for their wives. Williams describes Amanda as, "A little woman of great but confused vitality clinging frantically to another time and place," who "having failed to establish contact with reality, continues to live vitally in her illusions" (*ibid*, p. 129).

Removed into her past and needing to fortify an endangered sense of self-worth, Amanda assumes an archaic form of southern behavior, gentility. In the early American South a genteel code developed, giving the white southern woman homage both to safeguard her purity from the manhood of black slaves and to symbolize a civilizing influence on the decadent ways of the white landed gentry (Cash, *The Mind of the South*, pp. 87-9). So "gentlemen callers" represent a time when men were chivalrous and women were respected, admired, and pampered. Amanda affects the pose of superiority granted by this code to women, along with the flirtatiousness of the genteel lady who could attract and allure, giving a man hopes of reward without committing herself.

Amanda can act as the southern belle, but when she tries to force the role on Laura, the result is a complete disintegration of Laura's personality. She has precariously managed to protect herself from what she regards as a harsh and judgmental world by making her own world out of old records and tiny glass figurines. Laura's retreat from the real world is a result of her belief that since she is crippled, she is unlovely and unloveable. Feeling unattractive, Laura is frightened by a situation in which this attractiveness is directly tested, entertaining a man. Her self-consciousness and introversion thus reach a climax during her evening with Jim, the gentleman caller.

Unable to act like Amanda, Laura eventually responds to Jim's warmth. She forgets herself as they talk and even trusts him with the unicorn, a symbol for herself. But after Jim kisses her and then apologizes because he is engaged, Laura immediately retreats for protection into her inner world: "She rises unsteadily and crouches beside the Victrola to wind it up" (Vol. I, p. 231, *Theatre*). Her distorted sense of reality prevents the realization that Jim's actions have nothing to do with her attractiveness. Self-centered for too long, she seems incapable of realizing that what comes into her world does not necessarily reflect on her. Given such a limited perception, Laura cannot participate in human relationships and will continue to be unhappy in the real world.

Blanche resembles both Amanda and Laura in her reactions to the harsh world. Her attempt to hold the crumbling world of the family plantation together is similar to Amanda's attempt to keep her family together. Also like Amanda, she refuses to accept the reality of her life and attempts to live under illusion. She has a false sense of gentility which is contradicted by an equally false flight to promiscuity. The conflict between these two modes of behavior means self-defeat instead of survival. At the play's end, Blanche can only retreat into an insanity that exceeds Laura's withdrawal.

Blanche's moment of crisis occurred when she discovered her husband was a homosexual and in a moment of disgust drove him to suicide. The memory recurs in vivid flashes to haunt Blanche who only wants to avoid the "blinding light." She does not want to face her rejection of her husband and the part she played in his suicide.

Criticism of Stella's sordid condition allows Blanche to forget her own unhappy life. She refuses to believe that Stella has adjusted to this new way of life which is so different from the plantation world where women were ladies. It is the "lady" that is speaking when Blanche judges Stanley, Stella's husband, as beneath them because he is not a gentleman. Blanche's attempt to maintain the image of herself as a correct and genteel lady also leads her to deny her real sexual nature. Blanche too pines for the "gentleman" who will rescue her.

Blanche's sexual nature asserts itself, however, contrary to her attempts at gentility, and this leads to her breakdown. She avoids adult sexual relationships but actively seeks affairs with adolescents. She has just been exiled from her hometown because she attempted to seduce a boy. She later admits that she has had many "one-night stands" with the young soldiers of the nearby army camp. And the stage action shows her urge to seduce a young newspaper boy. Blanche seeks relationships with boys both because she feels guilty about the death of her young husband and because she is sexually immature and inadequate. Though she does not wish for the complications of love, panic drives her to sex when her memories have made existence intolerable: "After the death of Allan — intimacies with strangers was all I seemed able to fill my empty heart with . . . I think it was panic, just panic, that drove me from one to another, hunting for some protection . . ." (*ibid*, p. 386). After all, Blanche says, the opposite of death is desire.

Blanche's real motive for pursuing sexual relationships, however, seems to be the one she cannot face, her sexual inadequacy. Allan, she says, "came to me for help. I didn't know that . . . . all I knew was I'd failed him in some mysterious way . . ." (*ibid*, p. 354). It is this failure that Blanche is trying to exorcise by forming relationships with boys. She might be able to satisfy one of them in a way she was never able to satisfy her boyish husband Allan. This sense of inadequacy also accounts for her acute awareness of her physical attractiveness. She exercises her sexual charm to prove her allure — not for sexual gratification. Fearing that she will be unable to win a man and knowing that failure will mean she will have to face herself, Blanche pursues Mitch. But she has no wish for a mature man-woman relationship and never really views Mitch as a sexual conquest. Blanche's feelings for Mitch are totally self-centered. She sees him as "a cleft in the rock of the world that I could hide in!" (*ibid*, p. 387). She wants him to protect her from her persistent vision of Allan's suicide: "You've stopped that polka tune that I had caught in my head" (*ibid*, p. 380).

Stanley, in his ignorance and insensitivity, destroys both Blanche's hope and her illusion. He sees through her pose without understanding why she needs one. He thinks merely that she feels superior to him, and he wishes to destroy her composure to make her recognize that she is the same as he, a sexual animal. Stanley takes Blanche's teasing as a sign of real sexuality and concludes that they've "had this date with each other from the beginning!" (*ibid*, p. 402). The rape shatters Blanche's desperate pose for dignity and also forces on her what she is inadequate to endure, raw sexual passion. The result is insanity.

Blanche's sister, Stella, deals with reality in a basically healthy way. Rather than holding on to the old way of life at Belle Reve, she left to make her own living. Survival is always self-centered, however, as Blanche knows when she accuses Stella of deserting the family. Stella ignores the needs of others and eventually adopts her own illusion. Life with Stanley — sex with Stanley — is her highest value. Her refusal to accept Blanche's story of the rape is a commitment to self-preservation rather than love, and thus Stella contributes to Blanche's disintegration.

In *Summer and Smoke* written in 1948 Williams' characterization of women begins to change. Alma, unlike the heroines of the early plays who reject reality, develops in the course of the play from a woman who lives in the illusion of impossible aspiration and idealism into a woman who accepts reality and who actively seeks what she wants. Concurrent with this development, she grows in her capability to communicate with others. She overcomes her egocentrism and self-pity and offers kindness to someone in need.

The crisis that leads to this change in Alma is her complex feelings about herself and her life during this summer of her middle twenties. She feels that her youth is passing and knows that she is already considered an old maid. She resents the need to care for a senile and selfish mother and a self-pitying father: "I have had certain difficulties and disadvantages to cope with — which may be partly the cause of the peculiarities of mine . . ." (Vol. II, p. 152, *Theatre*). Then John Buchanan, the boy whom Alma has always loved, returns and disturbs Alma with his rejection of her idealism and his insistence on the physical nature of relationships between a man and a woman.

Highly idealistic behavior has always come naturally to Alma since she is the daughter of a minister. Even as a ten-year-old child she was adultlike, dignified with a quality of spirituality, and intrigued by the idea of eternity. These characteristics have intensified with age. The playwright says, "An excessive propriety and self-consciousness is apparent in her nervous laughter . . ." (*ibid*, p. 135). Alma's daydreams about eternity have solidifed into a philosophy of otherworldliness. The symbol of her idealism is the Gothic cathedral because "everything seems to be straining for something out of the reach of stone — or human — fingers." Life, to Alma, is "the everlasting struggle and aspiration for more than our human limits have placed in our reach." Man lives in the gutter, she believes, but "some of us are looking at the stars" (*ibid*, p. 197).

This idealism is illusionary, however, because Alma has been unable to translate it into positive action. Her care of her mother leads her to self-pity. She is bitter because she has not gotten anything for her sacrifice, not even recognition. Her life tied to duty, Alma has a dream about what she would do if things were different. She says to John, "Most of us have no choice but to lead useless lives! But you . . . have a chance to serve humanity. Not just to go on enduring for the sake of endurance, but to serve a noble, humanitarian cause, to relieve human suffering" (*ibid*, p. 154).

Alma also has an exalted notion of the role of woman as wife and mother. She thinks a woman must bring her heart and soul to marriage, and she rejects sexuality as often no better than bestiality. She rejects John's anatomy lesson: "I reject your opinion of where love is, and the kind of truth you believe the brain to be seeking! — There is something not shown on the chart" (*ibid*, p. 221). Alma, of course, means the soul. John sees this ideal as another example of Alma's Gothic cathedral image of life and suggests that Alma would never be satisfied with a normal love relationship; she would be striving for the impossible. Alma admits that her attempts to establish relationships with men have all failed because of "a desert between us" (*ibid*, p. 198). She has never been able to care for any man: "None of them really engaged my serious feelings" (*ibid*, p. 200). The one man Alma loves, John, she has loved with her soul, but he rejects this love. It is, he tells her, actually what kept him away from her: "The night at the casino — I wouldn't have made love to you . . . I'm more afraid of your soul than you're afraid of my body. You'd have been as safe as the angel of the fountain — because I wouldn't feel *decent* enough to touch you . . ." (*ibid*, p. 222).

With the impact of her whole situation and with John's rejection, Alma is forced to see that her idealism does not lead to positive acts in her own life. After a period of physical collapse and mental turmoil, she decides to pursue personal fulfilment. She decides that a person "can ask for the coming true of his most impossible dreams" (*ibid*, p. 241). Her old self is dead: "the girl who said 'no,' she doesn't exist any more" (*ibid*, p. 243). Though Alma realizes that she can no longer marry John, she reveals her new strength when she goes to him to declare that she loves him: "I haven't come here on any but equal terms . . . . It's no longer a secret that I love you. It never was" (*ibid*, p. 245). She does not indulge in self-pity. She attempts to understand what has happened to her former relationship with John and, unselfishly, hides her tears rather than detract from Nellie's happiness.

In the last scene, Alma is administering to a lonely and nervous traveling salesman. She has lost her extreme propriety; she laughs naturally and engages in light banter. Unencumbered by a false ideal of what love should be, she is ready to accept another for what he is and make the most of this human contact. This may not be a relationship "to engage her serious feelings," but it is a relationship that springs from a new genuineness and a clearer view of reality. In earlier plays women were able to find relief from emotional crises only in illusion, but in *Summer and Smoke* and the subsequent plays of the fifties except for *Orpheus Descending* Williams portrays women able to face reality and enjoy healthier relationships.

In *The Rose Tattoo*, Williams depicts Serafina, who with a "woman's heart passionately in love" (*ibid*, p. 270), idealizes her marriage with Rosario. To her, married sex is the ultimate experience, "a religion," and she is proud of her adherence to its values: faithfulness, chastity, and purity. But the idea that making love had consecreated her and her husband is an illusion because Rosario was not faithful, and there is no indication that he even loved Serafina. After his death, she continues to exalt his memory and maintains her idealization of their relationship. In order to do this, she cloisters herself from the real world. Putting her "heart in the marble urn with the ashes" (*ibid*, p. 372), she quits taking care of herself, lives in the past, and talks to the ashes.

When Serafina learns after years of homage that Rosario defiled their marriage bed, she is freed from her illusion. She does not react as Amanda does to her husband's desertion. Instead the truth frees Serafina from adoration of a memory. She is saved from despair by Alvaro to whom she turns in a relationship so practical that it cannot be idealized. He admits the economic advantages of marriage with Serafina, but at the same time he offers "Love and affection! — in a world that is lonely — and cold!" (*ibid*, p. 366). Serafina comes through her crisis to realize, like Alma that life is too important to reject for a memory.

Unlike Serafina, Maggie of *Cat on a Hot Tin Roof* has no illusions at the time of the play. Instead she is clear about her two main goals: to acquire money and to overcome her estrangement from Brick. She says she wants money so she can take care of Brick, and she refuses to leave him because she loves him. It is difficult to believe her motivation is other-centered, however, because of information which indicates how selfishly she acted in her earlier days. She forced Brick to marry her; and then when she saw Skipper as a threat to her relationship with Brick, she accused him of homosexuality even though she knew it would be devastating to him. She admits she acted wrongly since she now knows Brick desires only the most ideal relationship. Her self-centeredness has caused her to act in illusion.

Maggie is motivated in part by a background of genteel poverty. Growing up, she felt inferior because her family had to struggle to maintain a respectable standard of living despite an alcoholic father. Maggie resented the rich relatives who expected her fondest gratitude in exchange for castoff possessions. Now she says she must have money to feel good in old age.

The effect of this information is to make all her actions ambiguous. When she manipulates everyone around her in her competition with Mae and Gooper for Big Daddy's estate, she may only want the money for herself. On the other hand, she may be acting out of love for Brick, as she says. No matter for what reasons, when she uses Brick's alcoholism to accomplish her ends, her actions can only appear destructive. This ambiguity is compounded because whatever Maggie does for her husband, she ultimately does for herself as well. Securing an inheritance will benefit them both. An emotionally whole Brick will be a better lover for Maggie.

Two elements of the play, Maggie's identification with Big Mama and the revised act three, indicate the author's intention and resolve our questions. Big Mama and Maggie have similar relationships with their husbands. Both love the same type of man; Big Daddy is just an older version of Brick. Williams says he "must have had something Brick has, who made himself loved so much by the 'simple expedient' of not loving enough to disturb his charming detachment, also once coupled, like Brick's, with virile beauty" (Vol III, p. 138-39, *Theatre*). And both women are misunderstood by their husbands who find it hard to believe in their love. When their wives declare their love, both men respond with the same words, "Wouldn't it be funny if that was true?" (*ibid*, pp. 78, 166). Big Mama's joy that Daddy will live, her anguish when she learns the truth, her refusal to let the children appropriate his power, and her hurt when she sees that Big Daddy does not know how much she loves him all demonstrate that she loves unselfishly. By identifying Maggie with Mama, Williams shows he thinks Maggie is a lover too.

The revision of the third act further explains Maggie's character. Elia Kazan influenced the changes to show a Maggie who is less ambiguous in her actions because he wanted her character to be "more clearly sympathetic to an audience." Williams accepted this suggestion "wholeheartedly" because Maggie "had become steadily more charming to me as I worked on her characterization" (*ibid*, p. 168). As a result, the Maggie that emerges is no longer as manipulative or destructive to others.

Maggie seems genuinely concerned about Big Mama when she calls Brick to comfort her. Whereas in the original play Maggie called Brick only at Mama's bidding, several lines of dialogue have been added to show that Maggie anticipates Big Mama's need for comfort and support against Mae and Gooper and their plans. She says to Brick, "they're going to tell Big Mama the truth now, an' she needs you!" (*ibid*, p. 174). Maggie even uses a threat: "I'm going to take every dam' bottle on this place an' pitch it off th' levee into th' river!" (*ibid*, p. 179) — to make Brick respond. In the original, when Maggie used this threat, she was manipulating a helpless man. Here Brick is strong enough that he is not threatened and hears her words as a sign of vitality and determination.

The other major change in the action grows from Brick's self-realization. In the Broadway version the changes in Brick's awareness of his guilt is immediate, and so he is less defensive toward Maggie. He is able to respect her vitality and he accepts her aid. When Maggie maneuvers to defeat the ambitions of Mae and Gooper with news of her pregnancy, Brick gives her support. The revised last scene also suggests that Brick responds with love to Maggie. Encountering the thoroughness of her determination, he does not abjectly give up with nothing to say. Rather, he says, "I admire you, Maggie' (*ibid*, p. 214). The stage action shows his willingness to turn out the lights and begin their lovemaking. His receptiveness makes Maggie's final speech ring true: "Oh, you weak, beautiful people who give up with such grace. What you need is someone to take hold of you — gently, with love, and hand your life back to you . . . and I can! I'm determined to do it . . ." (*ibid,* p. 215). Maggie is a vital woman who can be misunderstood, but the weight of the play tends to move our understanding of her as a person who, if responsive to her own needs, is at least equally responsive to the needs of other persons around her.

Unlike Maggie, the women in *Orpheus Descending* are so

involved in trying to survive in a hostile and violent society that they have no strength left for healthy relationships. Vee Talbot, the sheriff's wife, faces the cruelty and violence of the county jail. She sees "awful things take place" (*ibid*, p. 291): beatings, lynchings, runaway convicts torn to pieces by dogs. Moral corruption marks the society which spawns such violence. The women are backbiters and adulterers; the men are intolerant and sadistic.

Vee believes she has a mission to help people, to "save" them, to "build up characters!" but the townspeople scorn her religiosity. Confused by the world of light and shadow, religion and hatred, which she inhabits, Vee turns to her paintings as a method of survival. Denying the appearances of the world as misleading, she believes visions are the only way to see and so paints under their influence. Val articulates her feelings about her art best when he says, "You make some beauty out of this dark country" (*ibid*, p. 292). Her creativity leaves her exhausted but elevated above and purified of the gross world. Her paintings are an escape into fantasy which eventually blind her totally to the real world.

Carol, a member of an aristocratic family in the town, tried to struggle singlehandedly against its cruelty and injustice. She delivered speeches, wrote letters, and protested against the injustices done to the black people by the white minority. She says, "I thought it was wrong for pellagra and slow starvation to cut them down when the cotton crop failed from army worm or boll weevil or too much rain in summer" (*ibid*, p. 251). So she used her inheritance to set up free clinics. Then when a black man was electrocuted "for having improper relations with a white whore" (*ibid*, p. 252), she personally protested by setting off for the capital, in winter, dressed in a potato sack. The reaction of the town was to hoot, jeer, spit at her, and arrest her for lewd vagrancy.

Her economic resources bankrupt and her personal sense of well-being threatened by the rejection of her family and community, Carol employs bizarre survival tactics. Having people talk about her is one way of knowing she is alive, and so she irritates the populace: "I want to be noticed, seen, heard, felt! I want them to know I'm alive!" (*ibid*, p. 251). Movement gives her a sense of life so her life now is the endless, restless round of "jooking," driving, drinking, dancing, and lovemaking. She uses sex, even though it is painful and potentially dangerous, just "to be not alone, even for a few moments" (*ibid*, p. 282). Because she sees contact with another person as a way to feel alive, Carol's idea of a relationship is holding onto another for all she's worth. She says, "What on earth can you do on this earth but catch at whatever comes near you, with both your hands, until your fingers are broken?" (*ibid*, p. 245). Carol is too threatened to be able to forget herself and love another for his own sake.

Lady also lives with the effects of small town hatred and intolerance. Her father was burned to death in the fire set to teach him a lesson because "he sold liquor to niggers" (*ibid*, p. 232). Then Lady was rejected by her lover for a woman with social status and wealth. Badly hurt, she gave up on life and "sold" herself to a loveless marriage. Yet, she believes life has some meaning. She tells Val there is more to life than corruption, because "If I thought that was the answer I'd take Jabe's pistol or his morphine tablets" (*ibid*, p. 273). Lady does not want to die and so she tries to begin living again. She wants to open a replica of her father's wine garden in the confectionery of the Torrence store. In this way, she will reassert her father's presence and her own identity in the face of the town's resistance. She hopes to overcome David's rejection and regain self esteem by reviving the richness of the time when he loved her. She tells him, "don't pity me . . . in there's the confectionery which'll reopen this spring, . . . it's going to be like — the wine garden of my father, those wine-drinking nights when you had something better than anything you've had since!" (*ibid*, p. 286). When Lady learns that Jabe was the leader of the Mystic Crew the night her father was burned out, the revival becomes "necessary, it's just something's got to be done to square things away . . . . *Just to be not defeated!*" (*ibid*, p. 329).

This single ambition to endure consumes Lady. She will use any means to obtain her end, including Val. She begs him to stay with her, not because she loves him, but because she needs him "TO LIVE . . . . TO GO ON LIVING!!!" (*ibid*, p. 305). When the situation in the town threatens him and he wants to leave, Lady selfishly keeps him with her, promising that they will go after she has had her revenge. Then when she realizes she is pregnant, Lady does not need Val anymore and tells him to leave. She has life now and is self-sustaining. It seems an inconsistency when she covers Val with her body and takes her husband's bullets. This self-sacrificing behavior is out of line with her pattern of survival.

None of the women in *Orpheus Descending* achieves even the readiness for compassionate love. A sense of acceptance of and survival in the real world must come first. Williams' characters in the fifties generally attain these qualities. This play is an exception possibly because it is a reworking of a play of 1940, *Battle of Angels*.

In *The Night of the Iguana*, Williams repeats in the character of Hannah Jelkes the basic theme that facing reality may develop compassion. Williams says, "She suggests a Gothic cathedral image of a medieval saint, but animated . . . . she is totally feminine and yet androgynous-looking — almost timeless" (Vol IV, p. 266, *Theatre*). Hannah's femininity takes the form of the comforting mother figure, as Shannon perhaps realizes when he calls her "Miss . . . Thin-Standing-Up-Female-Buddha" (*ibid*, p. 346). She does, in any case, immediately respond to Shannon's obvious need for compassion.

Hannah is compassionate because she has endured her own personal crisis and is able to sympathize with the confusion and panic of others. She tells Shannon: "I can help you because I've been through what are you going through now . . . I showed [my spook] that I could endure him and I made him respect my endurance" (*ibid*, pp. 352-53). Hannah has saved herself from passive existence in a dream world by controlling her panic: "I never cracked up, I couldn't afford to . . . . My work, this occupational therapy that I gave myself — painting and doing quick character sketches — made me look out of myself, not in, and gradually, at the far end of the tunnel that I was struggling out of I began too this faint, very faint grey light — the light of the world outside me — and I kept climbing toward it" (*ibid*, p. 355). The experience has made her feel that people need "A little understanding exchanged between them, a wanting to help each other through nights like this" (*ibid*, p. 352). Despite her own immediate problems with her grandfather's illness and their penury, Hannah acts on her belief that people can "see and know each other" and "if they're decent . . . help each other all that they can" (*ibid*, p. 324).

Hannah's kindness contrasts with the sensual egocentrism

of Maxine, "a stout, swarthy woman in her middle forties — affable and rapaciously lusty" (*ibid*, p. 255). She demands male attention and seeks it from Shannon as well as the Mexican boys. Maxine thinks she has no illusions. She says to Shannon, "I know the difference between loving someone and just sleeping with someone — even I know about that. We've both reached a point where we've got to settle for something that works for us in our lives — even if it isn't on the highest kind of level" (*ibid*, p. 329). However, her willingness to substitute immediate gratification for human contact and creative love make her weaker than Hannah who always seeks the human contact. In fact, Maxine's sexual drives lead to her false assessment of the relationship between Hannah and Shannon as sexual. "I got the vibrations between you . . .," she says, "and there sure was a vibration between you and Shannon the moment you got here. That, just that, believe me, nothing but that has made this . . . misunderstanding between us" (*ibid*, p. 322). As a result, Maxine wants to send Hannah and her grandfather, who is hardly able to travel, away from the hotel. Maxine's sexual drives make her selfish, deluded, and unkind.

Examination of Williams' women characters shows that over-simplified classifications are inadequate. Williams gradually characterized women to dramatize the theme that a woman must avoid illusions about both herself and others. Amanda is too involved in illusion to see her daughter's mental condition, and Laura is too involved in self to love. Blanche has failed once at love and spends the rest of her life trying to avoid it. Stella's sexuality leads her to choose illusion and life with Stanley rather than truth and love for Blanche. Later, women face reality and so acquire the capacity to be loving. Alma is saved from lovelessness by the realization that her false idealism prevents her from making real contact with others. Serafina is on the way to a healthier relationship when she realizes she has over-idealized married sex and withdrawn from life. Maggie is so vital that she is not subject to illusion for long, and she eventually attains unselfish behavior.

In all these plays, sexuality has been present but not necessarily the primary ingredient in the relationships. In *The Night of the Iguana* Williams makes a clear statement that sexuality is not a necessary prerequisite to a loving relationship. Hannah is not sexual, but she is totally selfless and responsive to the needs of others. On the other hand, Maxine's sexuality makes her self-centered. Clearly, Williams indicates the independence of human compassion from human sexuality and, more importantly, the interdependence of love and understanding. The women who idealize reality retreat into an illusionary world. They use bizarre behavior because they cannot accept themselves or others. Women who face reality are in the middle ground, committed to the here and now, and vital. Their desire to live may eventually be selfish or loving. The women who are realists and who sympathize with others and their problems are the truly compassionate. Williams has called himself an old romanticist. Judging by the plays considered, by "romanticist" he must mean one who believes in the power of love; and the fullest love, as Williams shows, is compassion formed only in reality.

Review Questions and Answers

The following questions and answers are provided to suggest the kinds of essay questions you may encounter and to frame one possible answer to each. The questions have been designed to be representative — there are many ways to ask the same kinds of questions about literary works. A question relating to imagery or symbol might be asked about other images and symbols than those shown here. A question about dramaturgy that focuses on irony or the effectiveness of a scene might just as easily be asked about dramatic language or a specific dramatic device like a soliloquy. You should read the questions and their answers not with blind faith but with skepticism and with interpretations of your own. The answers given below are test-formatted, that is, without the full documentation that you would need in a term, research, or take-home paper. Where documentation is lacking or where your own reading produces conclusions different from the ones you read here — that is the best place to become critical. Additional questions are provided in the section which follows, but without answers, for your own practice.

Question 1.

Costumery, like language and music, has an important symbolic role in the play, particularly the clothing worn by Stanley and Blanche. Discuss the symbolic use of clothing so as to suggest how Williams uses this device to tie together some of his major themes.

Answer 1.

Clothing in *Streetcar* is carefully chosen so that it serves many purposes all at once — color for stunning visual effects, kinds of clothing to show something about inner character of the wearer, and symbolic clothing to suggest a deeper significance to the action of the play. The characters themselves think of clothing in symbolic terms, particularly Stanley and Blanche, whose raging conflict extends to their respective wardrobes. In their clothes can be seen such major themes as illusion, pride, zest for life, confinement and imprisonment, ostentation, sexuality, and social class.

Stanley's dress is a reflection of the contradictions in his personality from the defiantly vulgar dress he wears at home to the resplendently colored and even prideful clothing he wears to the bowling alley. For all of his criticisms of Blanche's wardrobe, his own conscious use of the brilliant silk pyjamas — which he wore on his wedding night — in his deliberate rape of Blanche outruns all her less conscious manipulations. The brilliant color of Stanley's pyjamas reminds the viewer of his parade of brightly coloured shirts — including the one Stella tore when confronting him with his cruelty after the miserable birthday party for Blanche. Animal pride and a wish to display merge with carnality, cruelty, and the killing instinct in Stanley's rape of Blanche.

Blanche's complexity is also mirrored in her dress. Her pure white garden-party suit at the opening of the play is completely wrong for the Elysian Fields. Her entire wardrobe is designed to project an image — the one Stanley is at first fooled by — of upper-class wealth. But her tiara is made of rhinestones, and some of her better clothes and perfume are old gifts. Blanche's concern is for appearance, for the effects she can create to achieve her ends. She has Stanley zip up her dress, and she receives Mitch in her dressing gown. Clothing for her, as for Stanley, is a necessary part of the arsenal of sexual dominance. Ironically, in the end there is mention of a straight-jacket for Blanche, a garment that is unnecessary since she is already safely bound up in her illusions. She departs on the doctor's arm as if he offers the security Shep Huntleigh represents in her fantasies.

Blanche's final appearance brings together the clothing imagery that has surrounder her through the play. She at first appears in a red satin robe, an emblem of the carnality pressed upon her by Stanley and a reminder of her connection with him through his own brightly colored clothing. Then she changes very consciously into a dress of Della Robia blue, "The blue of the robe in the old Madonna pictures." Still against the facts, she dreams of her virginal purity, a Virgo to the end, and in the Madonna robe foresees her own death as if to herald the arrival of the personnel from the state institution.

Question 2.

The moral code regarding sexuality for women in *Streetcar* is fairly clear. Even though it may not seem fair, Blanche,

Stella, and Eunice all offer some perspective on it and seem to accept it. Less clear is the moral code for men. Explore the male code with specific reference to Stanley, Mitch, and Allan to discover whether Williams has an implicit or explicit point of view on the matter.

Answer 2.

Males, no less than females, labor in an environment of social code and taboo in Williams' drama, but the male code is complex, presented through a range of characters, some present and others only remembered. Male sexuality in *Streetcar* is not limited to Stanley Kowalski, even though he is the most powerfully presented male. His rape of Blanche is criminal and inhuman. The fact that he quickly seeks atonement each time he abuses his wife and places his unborn child at risk in no way exonerates him. As Williams implies by Mitch's ineffectual lunge at Stanley at the end of the play, other types of males exist, but unfortunately Stanley's type prevails.

Mitch, still capable of romantic love, has the same attitudes as Stanley about marrying only a young virgin. When he discovers the truth about Blanche's immediate past, he does not care to look for explanations. Within the play's world, Shaw, Kiefaber, Graves, Stanley, and, by implication, nearly every male in normal society would agree with Mitch's viewpoint. Mitch had an early tragic attachment and continues to be influenced by his sick mother (who shares his views and clarifies them for him). He is not refined in the cultural sense but, as Blanche instinctively knows, he is an idealist and can treat women with a respect that is a laughing matter to his coarse friends.

Mitch and Allan are Blanche's two attempts at a potentially workable long-term relationship with a man. Where Mitch discovers an ugly truth about Blanche, earlier Blanche discovered an ugly truth about her husband Allan — his homosexuality. More devastating than a woman's promiscuity to her reputation was the revelation of a man's homosexuality to his. Like Hart Crane, the poet whose work provided the epigram to the play, Allan was a poet who committed suicide. Blanche keeps his letters and poems in a bundle in her trunk and thinks they are defiled when Stanley touches them. Allan's memory comes alive for Blanche whenever she considers an experience with a man; Allan for her not only means a level of refinement she can't find in the real world but also a tragic end filled with violence and horror.

Shep Huntleigh and the doctor from the asylum are, like Mitch, representatives of the safe and peaceful world that Blanche hopes men will provide. For Blanche, this aspect of maleness is as devoid of both sex and love. This aspect of Blanche's psyche was unknown to Allan, despite his apparent sensitivity. Taboo and shame overruled all his other impulses and led to tragedy.

Williams' point of view is not entirely objective. His sympathy for males is limited to Mitch and to Allan. The raw sexuality we see in Stanley and in the parade of men at the Hotel Flamingo is little different from the female version of it we see in Stella and Eunice.

Within the confines of the play, Williams leaves little doubt which males can survive and which cannot, and the code sanctions the survivors. But that code is severely questioned by implication. Allan, like Blanche, was destroyed by what he was in relation to society — an outsider of special vulnerability.

Question 3.

The climax of *Streetcar* is the rape of Blanche by Stanley, an event which ironically coincides with the birth of Stanley and Stella's baby. The two events are related and suggest the careful planning behind the play's structure. How does Williams use the technique of parallelism to give his play unity, complexity, and breadth?

Answer 3.

Parallelism is one of the main devices Williams uses to draw the complexities of life within the artificial confines of a stage play. In performance the device is difficult to detect because of the rapid pace of the action. But its effects are felt in the impression of wholeness and strength we sense afterwards. From relatively flat characters, contrived but powerful actions, and sometimes blatant symbols, Williams shapes a rich and dynamic environment. He does this by making characters, events and symbols mirror or contrast with each other. Because of how these parts connect with each other, the play suggests the presence of a web of order beneath the surface chaos of violence and sensuality. The principle of order that emerges is tragic. The parallel characters include the obvious example of Blanche and Stella, whose sisterhood provides a basis for comparison and for contrast. Both women have romantic, symbolic names; both are of a different social class than the rest of the play's characters. Yet Stella has opted for a style of life that her sister finds repellant. In fact, the two women have separate and distinct characters, nowhere better symbolized than in their relationships to Stanley.

The rape and insanity of Blanche are in contrast to the sensuality and childbearing of Stella. Eunice serves as a contrasting figure to both sisters; she lives an even more brutal life than Stella; her man is probably cheating on her at a local house and commands none of the limited regard of Blanche's men. Stanley, Mitch, Steve, and Pablo can all be compared and contrasted, and since they form a comfortable society, they imply a system of values belonging to a whole class of men.

Williams also builds parallel events both to heighten dramatic effect and to call attention to major themes. Blanche's rape, Stella's giving birth, Allan's suicide, and Blanche's final departure are part of the pattern of life-and-death violence in the play. Blanche expects Shep Huntleigh and the security of money to save her from poverty and a squalid existence but instead is escorted to an asylum (a different kind of security than she expected). On the one hand, Stella is pregnant and finally gives birth to a child who symbolizes the bond between herself and Stanley; on the other, Mitch's mother is sick and even in her sickness succeeds in cutting off an avenue of her son's future happiness by asking the question about Blanche's age. The birth pangs begin for Stella just after the birthday party for Blanche, and are curiously related to the pain that Stanley has caused and will cause Blanche.

Symbols and symbolic actions are also related, so consciously that Williams is often accused of being heavy-handed in their use. For example, Stanley's smashing light bulbs on his wedding night parallels his crushing the lantern that Blanche has placed over the light — the same lantern that Mitch took off the light when he wished to see the real Blanche for the first time. Mitch's silver case with its verse inscribed is a gift from a girl who loved him and died, and its counterpart is the treasured bundle of letters that Blanche keeps in her trunk. Both link the themes of refinement, love and death and show the kindred spirit of Mitch and Blanche. Stanley's symbolic acts of violence, which we see when he throws things (a package of meat, a radio, a plate) or bellows for Stella after injuring her, are in counterpoint to his investigative acts (the fate of Belle Reve, Blanche's background in Laurel, the appraisal of Blanche's wardrobe. But his impulse to dominate everyone and everything is clear in each of them. The succession of actions that make us question Blanche's sanity — the interlude with the collector, the dumb show with the prostitute and rolled drunk, the various musical and other noise indicators, the appearance of the blind Mexican woman — have the effect of highlighting the tension between the themes of appearance and reality. They do this by clouding the distinction between the two.

These clusters of parallels are used for both comparison and contrast. They suggest not only a poet's use of dramatic detail but also a submerged implication that the features may have a necessary as well as a logical relation. The parallelism in *Streetcar* emphasizes that Williams' characters have a destiny. Stanley's statement to Blanche just before the rape stands in contrast to Blanche's just after Mitch has acknowledged the bond of need between them. The passionate necessity of sex is clearly differentiated from the fleeting, God-given gift of love.

Question 4.

Communication, or the lack of it, can be a tragic problem, and in Williams' drama it is often connected to such dominant themes as alienation, violence, and illusion. Explore the problem of meaningful human communication as it is presented in the interplay between Mitch and Blanche in *Streetcar.*

Answer 4.

Neither Mitch nor Blanche is a comfortable communicator. Their discomfort signals their desperation to satisfy their separate needs. Because they are not young, their histories get in the way. Because they do not take their time, they establish a framework of falsehoods and illusions. Because they don't know how hard it is to base a lasting relationship on a momentary sharing of deep sympathy, they set themselves up for disappointment.

That society itself sets the rules of their game, which

deepens the effect of the final loss, for with the false ideal of courtly romantic love, failure is guaranteed.

Mitch has the sensitivity that Blanche is looking for, even if he lacks Shep Huntleigh's money. But his dependency on his ailing mother and on his lofty ideals of womanhood make his ideals seem to be borrowed. His dependency on Stanley — an uneasy relationship between a follower and a leader — tramples his attempt to relate to Blanche alone. In Scene 6 after Blanche has protested about Mitch's lifting her into the air, Mitch suggests that they might like to go out with Stanley and Stella. Blanche's teasing has confused him, and he seeks the comfort of participating second-hand in what he thinks is a healthy relationship between the Kowalskis.

Mitch thinks that there is real love between Stanley and Stella in spite of their violent outbreaks. Mitch does not have the strength of character or the intellect to clarify his thoughts. When he is finally convinced that Blanche has lied to him about her ideals, he is adamant about not marrying her and thinks he has the right to take her anyway. He is not at all resolute about his desires, and backs down. He shows hurt and bewilderment, while Stanley later takes the initiative and rapes Blanche.

Mitch knows that he cares for his mother and that he is attracted to something about Blanche. He is sensitive but not intellectual — in fact he is not even intelligent. He is passive. His speech is responsive; he doesn't lead any conversations. Blanche drives their speech just as she drives their relationship.

Without Stanley's intervention, Mitch probably would have married Blanche. His functioning as a receiver, rather than as a transmitter, has limited what he can know about others.

Mitch's reticence complements his politeness. Trained to do the "right thing" and afraid go much beyond what his mother and male friends dictate, Mitch is confined by his society, just as he is confined at work to the spare parts bench. His life is a narrow one which centers around his mother, his job, poker with the boys, and working out at the New Orleans Athletic Club. Even Mitch's history is limited. The girl who gave him the cigarette case remains a mystery. It is not at all clear what he thought of her, (though it *is* clear that Blanche does not draw him out on the matter and even avoids the topic).

Mitch is a man of few words. His vocabulary is simple and he speaks a sentence or a part of a sentence at a time. He seems to want to communicate but often gropes for something to say. Stella tells Blanche that Mitch is more sensitive than the other men who play poker with Stanley.

He is a bachelor, and as such is more private, more vulnerable, and less rounded.

His reticence around others is due also to his having to care for his sick mother and to his knowledge that he will be alone when she dies. His concerns about his own future are as important for him as the fact of his mother's imminent death. She has expressed concern that Mitch will not be "settled" before she dies, and this concern is mirrored in his own thoughts. In fact, this one point of communication between mother and son almost defines the relationship between the two.

Communication through words is often not adequate; if the right words are required for a satisfactory relationship, we don't find them in *Streetcar*. Mitch's entire relationship with the girl who died is contained not in words but in the symbol of the present she gave him when she knew that she was going to die. When Mitch tears the paper lantern off the light bulb, his statement about how he wants to see Blanche is very clear. Mitch communicates best through symbols, whether he is sharing cigarettes, perspiring through his shirt, carrying an inverted statue of Mae West (the sex symbol of that era), or showing up in his work clothes. In this way, he becomes the most human of all the characters in the play. His symbolic communication, with its brute honesty, is in stark contrast to the wide range of communication used by Blanche to communicate nothing.

Blanche was a professional communicator. She taught English in a high school. She has a French background and can speak a few lines of vulgar French. She can talk circles around Mitch; her technique is to engage his sympathy and admiration, to keep him off balance, to make him respect her; her goal is to get him to the altar.

Her description of Allan's tragic end is her first and best inroad to Mitch's heart. She becomes wholly absorbed in recalling that horrible evening at the Moon Lake Casino and for a moment forgets herself. She even accuses herself and reveals her abiding guilt. In that instant, the power of the story can break through her posing and Mitch's defenses. They mistake this fleeting moment of truth for the start of a relationship and the courtship begins in earnest.

When Blanche talks of "God" in one of her most moving and memorable lines (near the end of Scene 6 with Mitch), she means many things, but among them she means "hope," "communication," "sympathy" and "love." Neither Mitch nor Blanche can recapture this moment later, for its occurrence is almost miraculous. Its magic is in stark contrast to the "magic" we hear in Blanche's lies, and to the "magic" that Mitch equates with those "lies." The story of Allan's suicide is not precisely the point of Scene 6. What it signals is the deeper communication that happens through it. When Blanche later tries to remove her guilt by referring to the story, Mitch cannot understand.

Blanche often sees speech as entertainment. By means of speech the fearsome vacuum of silence is somehow compensated for. Her joke about the parrot at her birthday party is an example of speech to fill the void. Entertainment is not communication, only a poor substitute for it, or at best a holding pattern while we await the real thing. Like Blanche's bawdy French which she would be horrified to discover Mitch understands, her speech is meant not for understanding but — even worse — to block or stifle understanding when reality threatens.

Blanche complains about Mitch's inability to show her a good time on their date. She is really looking towards the marriage commitment — not a sexual commitment. Blanche's inability to accept what communication means is reflected in her inability to accept the brute reality of sex. She does not think of her relationships with Shep, Mitch, or Stanley in terms of sex, even though she pretends to parade herself as a sex object. Her coquetry is meant to entice but not deliver. Her use of herself as a symbol is flawed because she has no substantial meaning. Just as her language is designed to achieve the end of a marriage proposal, so her body language is designed to achieve admiration. Blanche does not see marriage even partly as a sexual match but only a safe harbor and a state of rest and comfort. For Mitch it has much the same meaning, and only when he has decided that he will not marry Blanche does he think of her as a means of immediate sexual gratification.

After the story about Allan (which roughly parallels the earlier story about the girl who gave Mitch the cigarette case), the only direct communication between Mitch and Blanche comes through symbols, chiefly the lighting used by Mitch to "illuminate" the real Blanche and the cries of "Fire!" by Blanche used to repel the now hated source of her disillusionment. Clearly, here the two characters speak in their separate "languages" with Mitch using physical symbols to complement his crude, blunt speech and with Blanche resorting to a terrible fiction (a house on fire) to be done with him.

The points of communication between Mitch and Blanche only highlight their inability to achieve some form of lasting communication. They will never be capable of entering into marriage with its give-and-take. The seemingly representative marriages shown in the play — those of Stanley and Stella or Steve and Eunice — with their alternating extremes of violence and robust animal-like gratifications, are beyond them. The flaws in sexuality visible in Mitch and Blanche serve to explain why they are still single and must remain so.

But vulnerability in this realm implies vulnerability in others. The social rules of the class above Stanley's will not permit meaningful communication, only entertainment, and Stanley's own class can communicate only through violence, including violent sexuality. This in turn implies a breakdown in language, values and symbols, and a division by class into those who must fail in trying to live a non-violent and refined life and those who do not even try. When Blanche accuses Stella of surrendering to animal instincts, she is right, and Stella virtually admits that the meaning in life for her is sex with Stanley. But Blanche cannot live a meaningful lifestyle without money, which in turn cannot be attained by any other means than marrying into the new version of lower-class American life. In both Stella's world and Blanche's, real communication has been cut off for both men and women. Mankind is left with an existence not far different from that of beasts, except that man can destroy himself or go insane (as happens to Allan and Blanche) if his sensitivity, or his illusion-building power, is violated.

Suggested Study Topics

The topics listed below may help you in organizing your thoughts about the play. You should not take as a task a written answer to each of the questions, but if you cannot begin to frame an answer to each one, you should go back to the play to see what you may have missed. The list, read in the order given, should make you recall most aspects of the play if you read it carefully more than once with notes. Confidence that you could tackle these questions in short essay questions or, with more time, in long ones, will probably indicate that you are ready to memorize a few quotations that might help in answering some of them.

It may seem like a formidable trial, but can you think of any additional questions that one could ask about the play? Make a list of your own questions, based on your class study or your own reading, and try to answer them. Any questions from below or from your list that you would have great trouble answering under pressure should be tried out on your friends or your teacher.

1. Explore Williams' use of colors to determine whether any large symbolic patterns emerge to complement such major themes in the play as death, love and pride. (One example is the silver of both Mitch's silver cigarette case and Blanche's silver-backed mirror, which are involved in themes of time, love, and loss.)
2. The staging of *Streetcar* is so carefully arranged in the author's directions that Williams seems to be using his space to the fullest. Trace how Williams uses his stage to test the limits of the medium.
3. Is *Streetcar* a play locked in a specific period of the American past? Has it any relevance for today's audience, or does it suggest something about the wider human condition? Whichever side you take, provide the best arguments for the opposite side and then refute them before presenting your case.
4. *Streetcar* is a play about the life struggle between two strong-willed sisters and between a strong-willed man and his sister-in-law. Defend or refute this assertion and document your proof.
5. Notice that many kinds of music are involved, both on and off the stage (for example, the Blue Piano, the trumpet, the

Varsouviana, Blanche's own singing, the radio music, allusions to music and musical taste, and the like). How does Williams use music to merge mood and meaning in the play?

6. Ethnic differences are pronounced in *Streetcar,* but are they central to the play's messages or only peripheral? Why are they so pronounced? Are they related to class divisions? (Do not focus exclusively on Stanley's being of Polish descent since this is the subject of another question listed below.)

7. Objects, even those that seem the most insignificant, often take on greater meaning in a Williams play (the plaster cast of Mae West, the silver mirror, and the like). Find a few additional physical objects that operate this way and associate them with a specific pattern of symbols or themes in the world. Try to show how they become powerful visual symbols in their own right without external reference.

8. Is Mitch justified in his treatment of Blanche? Is Stanley justified in his treatment of Mitch? In any case, what is Mitch's character and why is he an essential character in the play?

9. Are the Hubbells meant to be a humorous couple or a representative couple or a foil for the Kowalskis or some combination of these? How do they function in the play? Would anything be lost if they were deleted? How much is gained by their being included in the play?

10. Is Blanche raped or seduced? What is the effect, physical and symbolic, of Stanley's relation with her?

11. What does Shep Huntleigh represent for Blanche? Does Williams tell us anything about Blanche through her (both real and fantasy) relationship with him?

12. Gestation and birth is one of the dominant themes in the play. How does Williams interweave this theme with related and opposite themes to sharpen the ironies that make the drama come alive?

13. Does Williams take a moral stance in *Streetcar?* If so, what is it? If not, why not?

14. Relate the epigram (the excerpt from the poem by Hart Crane) to the action of the play. Is the epigram an adequate statement for the play as a whole?

15. A lot of drinking goes on in the play. Is the drinking just for color, or is a larger cluster of meanings suggested? Explore in detail.

16. Williams, like many other artists, wants both to

communicate his meaning and to make his communication exclusively through his art. Why, then, did he provide a preface to the play a few days prior to its first appearance? In what ways is the article a true vision — and in what ways is it a false one — of the creation and message of the play?

17. How are the stage and staging used to show us the thoughts and moods of Blanche DuBois?

18. What factors of social change in post-war southern America provide the basis for the larger setting of the play?

19. Stella and Stanley seem to be well-matched. What makes their relationship work? Or does it? How does Blanche's presence operate on the marriage? If you were Stella, how would you feel about someone like Blanche appearing as she does?

20. Blanche seems to have had an interesting sex life prior to her arrival in the Elysian Fields — but how much of what is "discovered" is really true, and what do Blanche's actions suggest about the rest?

21. Look up "neurasthenic" and use the definition given to test whether Williams means the term to suggest what is wrong with Blanche. Why does he use this term to describe her "condition"?

22. "Elysian Fields" are the fields of the blessed heroes of Greek mythology — dead heroes play there. In fact, the death theme is very strong in the play. But not one of the major visible characters dies. Discuss the theme of death as Williams explores it and, if you can, relate it to the question of whether the play is a tragedy or some other form of drama.

23. The original title of the play was *The Poker Night.* Why might that have been appropriate? What might have motivated Williams to change the title to *A Streetcar Named Desire?* Was the final title a wise choice?

24. Is *Streetcar* a natural imaginative sequel to the popular *The Glass Menagerie,* the work that catapulted Williams to fame? How do the plays compare? How do they differ?

25. Blanche's character is difficult to pin down because of her inconsistency. Often it seems as if she is more than one character or that she assumes a number of roles in succession. Discuss this idea of Blanche's complexity with specific reference to her insanity.

26. Choose the lines in the play that you think are most poetic.

What do they suggest about Williams' attitudes towards language? How do they compare with lines you consider the least poetic? Based on what you find, make a statement about Williams' range as a playwright.

27. In what ways is *Streetcar* a "memory play"? Relate your consideration to such themes as pain, love, sanity and death.

28. Physical contact occurs often on the stage during this violent play. How does Williams use this kind of action in other places than the rape scene?

29. Just as Stanley is rarely civil and almost never polite, so Blanche has none of the poise or genteel manners of the real Southern aristocracy. Defend or refute this.

30. Can you explain Blanche's attraction to Stanley? Could the sisters' roles have been reversed if Blanche had met Stanley first?

31. How do the Hotel Flamingo and the Four Deuces operate as offstage symbolic places? With whom are they associated? With what themes are they associated?

32. Would a jury acquit Stanley of rape? Document your answer fully with evidence drawn from the play.

33. What is the significance of the dumb show in which the prostitute rolls the drunk? How many other instances of similar intrusions on the dramatic action can you find? How is Williams using this kind of device in the play?

34. Is there any significance in Stanley being Polish? How is his Polishness used in the play? Could he have been from some other ethnic group with equal effectiveness? Is Blanche truly a bigot? Does Stanley confirm or cause doubt about the usual image of the Polish-American?

35. Originally the play was performed with intermissions after scene four and scene six. Is this a good division of the play? Why?

36. If you had too few actors to perform the play, which parts would you cut? (Assume you would have to cut four characters.) Justify your cuts by writing an apology to Williams himself (imagining him to be still alive).

37. In some ways the play is claustrophobic because of the close quarters of the main characters; in other ways the play is expansive, looking out on a whole landscape of American experience. Explain.

38. Discuss how the play might be interpreted as the battle of

Stanley and Blanche for the soul of Stella. Does the meaning of Stella's name have any significance in this consideration? Explain.

39. Blanche's literary and artistic allusions are often employed by her as weapons of attack or as vehicles of defence. Do any of the allusions have meanings she does not intend but which enrich the overall meaning of the play?

40. The bathroom is probably the most commented-on area of the Kowalski flat. Why does it get so much attention?

41. We associate soliloquies (speeches made by a character while alone or as if alone) with older traditional drama (Hamlet's famous "To be or not to be" soliloquy is one famous example). But Williams uses them liberally. Where do they occur in *Streetcar* and what is the dramatic reason for their use?

42. List all the occurrences of the paper lantern. Is there a pattern in the uses of the object? How does the lantern relate to the silver mirror that Blanche breaks just before the rape scene? What do both indicate about Blanche?

43. Animal imagery occurs with regularity throughout the play. Allusions to swine, a rooster, hens, apes, a lamb, a parrot, a tarantula, and others abound. What is its purpose? Is there another pattern of imagery that stands in opposition to this one? If there is, document it.

44. Show that Williams leaves nothing to chance in his stage directions by choosing a few seemingly insignificant details included there and demonstrating their importance in the play.

45. Off-color jokes are told by a number of people, to an assortment of reactions by the others present. Given that Williams does most things for a purpose, show their function in their separate contexts and then in the play as a whole. (One example is Blanche's joke about the parrot; another is Steve's about the rooster.)

46. Is there a pattern in the way Williams ends his scenes? Elaborate.

47. The media (radio, film, the telephone, the telegram) used in the play are limited but effective both as symbols and as dramatic devices. Just how does the post-war media environment effect the social life of the city dwellers of Stanley's class? Can you relate their use to such major themes as communication (or lack of it), alienation or violence?

48. Silence and whispers can be as effective as shouting or even more so. What evidence is there that Williams orchestrated the volume of speech? Say what he gains by the extremes of volume.

49. In a now-classical criticism of the play, Williams was accused of shallowness and profiteering in writing *Streetcar*. The critic stated that Williams only pretended to have a real message in the play but that his intention was to use the sure-fire formula of violence and sex to gain fame, prizes and money through notoriety and by fooling his viewers. In effect, this critic accused Williams of being even more of a fraud than Blanche because he was more conscious about what he was doing and less vulnerable. On what grounds do you suppose this allegation could be made? Do you agree with this critic, or can you find evidence that the play is, as other critics have suggested, profound and worthy of close attention?

50. Explain the meaning of the title of the play. But go beyond the fact that there really was a streetcar named Desire in New Orleans to the symbol itself?

51. Blanche said, "I saw. I know. You disgust me!" and her youthful and sensitive husband immediately went outside and blew his brains out. This event haunts her, coloring everything she thinks about love, or so it seems. Trace the twin themes of guilt and atonement, not just with respect to Blanche, but with respect to as many characters in the play as you can.

53. Read with great care Blanche's overheard diatribe against Stanley in Scene 4. This is an excellent example of irony of situation not only because Blanche is saying exactly what she least wants Stanley to hear, but also because of the result of her eloquence. How does Williams employ irony here to reveal character?

Bibliography

Although nearly every critic laments the enormous volume of critical material written about Williams, what they mean is that a lot of very good insights about the playwright and his plays are found in resources that are difficult to research. In this category are reviews of current productions, interviews with Williams that are available only in non-print media, and almost casual mention of a play in a volume about world drama or Southern literature or contemporary writers. The compilation by Gurr, listed below, is currently the best available, even though it does not say what each listed source contains. Other people have added to his list and, now that the playwright is dead, still more new sources will have to be added.

The plays of Williams have been published by New Directions, but these are not annotated to help the student today or the scholar tomorrow. The work on Williams' texts has not yet really begun.

Biography is also a problem area. Williams liked to talk and write *(Memoirs)* about himself; he left a wealth of sometimes contradictory and sometimes intentionally obscure data, and his unorthodox life-style forced him to be secretive and even mysterious. Many biographical accounts exist, and critics like to use Williams' biography to "explain" his plays, but the definitive biography has not yet been written, and studies of Williams' growth and development as an artist must await the good texts that will eventually be made.

Works that purport to discover Williams' psychology through his writings should be considered very suspect, even though using psychological tools to study the works themselves can sometimes be instructive. There is a whole school of psychological criticism of Williams which, together with the moral criticism, makes up most of the research done so far, but its quality is poor. The last word has not been written about Williams and, because of his complexity of design, very little of real value has emerged about his plays, except for the performances, which still engage audiences worldwide.

Donahue, Francis. *The Dramatic World of Tennessee Williams.* New York: Frederick Ungar, 1964.

Falk, Signi Lenea. *Tennessee Williams.* Second Edition. Boston: Twayne Publishers, 1978.

Gunn, Drewey Wayne. *Tennessee Williams: A Bibliography.* Scarecrow Author Bibliography, No. 48. Metuchen, New Jersey and London: The Scarecrow Press, 1980.

Hughes, Catherine R. *Tennessee Williams: A Biography.* Englewood Cliffs, New Jersey: Prentice-Hall, 1978.

Jackson, Esther Merie. *The Broken World of Tennessee Williams.* Madison: University of Wisconsin Press, 1965.

Law, Richard A. " 'A Streetcar Named Desire' as Melodrama," *English Record,* 14 (February, 1964), 2-8.

Leavitt, Richard F., ed. *The World of Tennessee Williams.* New York: G. P. Putnam's Sons, 1978 and London: W. H. Allen, 1978.

Londre, F. H. *Tennessee Williams.* New York: Frederick Unger, 1979.

Miller, Jordan Y., ed. *Twentieth Century Interpretations of* A Streetcar Named Desire: *A Collection of Critical Essays.* Englewood Cliffs, New Jersey: Prentice-Hall, 1971.

Nelson, Benjamin. *Tennessee Williams: The Man and His Work.* New York: Ivan Obolensky, 1961. and *Tennessee Williams: His Life and Work.* London: Peter Owens, 1961.

Stanton, S. S., ed. *Tennessee Williams.* Englewood Cliffs, New Jersey: Prentice-Hall, 1977.

Tharpe, Jac L., ed. *Tennessee Williams: A Tribute.* Jackson: University Press of Mississippi, 1977.

Tischler, Nancy M. *Tennessee Williams: Rebellious Puritan.* New York: Citadel Press, 1961.

Weales, Gerald. *Tennessee Williams.* Minneapolis: University of Minnesota Press, 1965.

NOTES

NOTES

NOTES

NOTES

NOTES